THE NEXT ADVENTURE

PILOT HUXLEY

DAN MCGUINESS

graphix

AN IMPRINT OF

M SCHOLASTIC

NEW YORK TORONTO LONDON AUCKLAND SYDNEY MEXICO CITY NEW DELHI HONG KONG

180-6102

FOR MY PARENTS, ELAINE AND BILL
M^cGUINESS. THANK YOU FOR SUPPORTING
ME IN EVERYTHING I'VE DONE.

TEXT AND ILLUSTRATIONS COPYRIGHT © 2011 BY DAN M^cGUINESS
ORIGINAL DESIGN BY DAN M^cGUINESS AND CLARE OAKES
COVER DESIGN BY PHIL FALCO

ALL RIGHTS RESERVED. PUBLISHED BY GRAPHIX, AN IMPRINT OF SCHOLASTIC INC.,
PUBLISHERS SINCE 1920. SCHOLASTIC, GRAPHIX, AND ASSOCIATED LOGOS ARE
TRADEMARKS AND/OR REGISTERED TRADEMARKS OF SCHOLASTIC INC.

NO PART OF THIS PUBLICATION MAY BE REPRODUCED, STORED IN A RETRIEVAL SYSTEM,
OR TRANSMITTED IN ANY FORM OR BY ANY MEANS, ELECTRONIC, MECHANICAL,
PHOTOCOPYING, RECORDING, OR OTHERWISE, WITHOUT WRITTEN PERMISSION OF THE
PUBLISHER. FOR INFORMATION REGARDING PERMISSION, WRITE TO SCHOLASTIC INC.,
ATTENTION: PERMISSIONS DEPARTMENT, 557 BROADWAY, NEW YORK, NY 10012.

FIRST PUBLISHED BY OMNIBUS BOOKS, A DIVISION OF SCHOLASTIC
AUSTRALIA PTY LIMITED, IN 2010.

THIS EDITION PUBLISHED UNDER LICENSE FROM SCHOLASTIC AUSTRALIA PTY LIMITED.

LIBRARY OF CONGRESS CONTROL NUMBER AVAILABLE

ISBN 978-0-545-26845-5
10 9 8 7 6 5 4 3 2 1   11 12 13 14 15
PRINTED IN THE U.S.A.   40
FIRST EDITION, SEPTEMBER 2011

CHAPTER ONE
THE VOID HOPPER

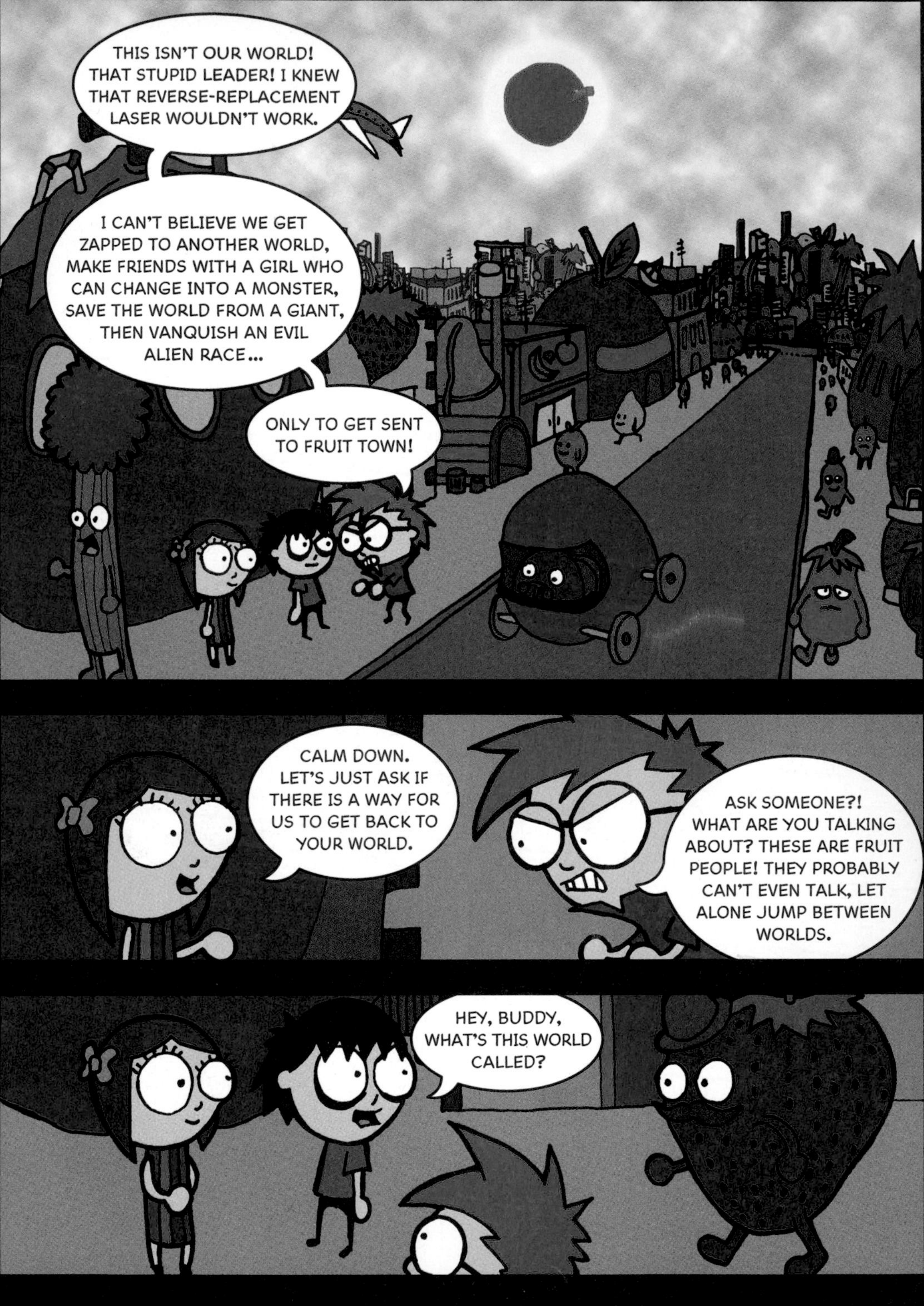
THIS ISN'T OUR WORLD! THAT STUPID LEADER! I KNEW THAT REVERSE-REPLACEMENT LASER WOULDN'T WORK.
I CAN'T BELIEVE WE GET ZAPPED TO ANOTHER WORLD, MAKE FRIENDS WITH A GIRL WHO CAN CHANGE INTO A MONSTER, SAVE THE WORLD FROM A GIANT, THEN VANQUISH AN EVIL ALIEN RACE...
ONLY TO GET SENT TO FRUIT TOWN!
CALM DOWN. LET'S JUST ASK IF THERE IS A WAY FOR US TO GET BACK TO YOUR WORLD.
ASK SOMEONE?! WHAT ARE YOU TALKING ABOUT? THESE ARE FRUIT PEOPLE! THEY PROBABLY CAN'T EVEN TALK, LET ALONE JUMP BETWEEN WORLDS.
HEY, BUDDY, WHAT'S THIS WORLD CALLED?

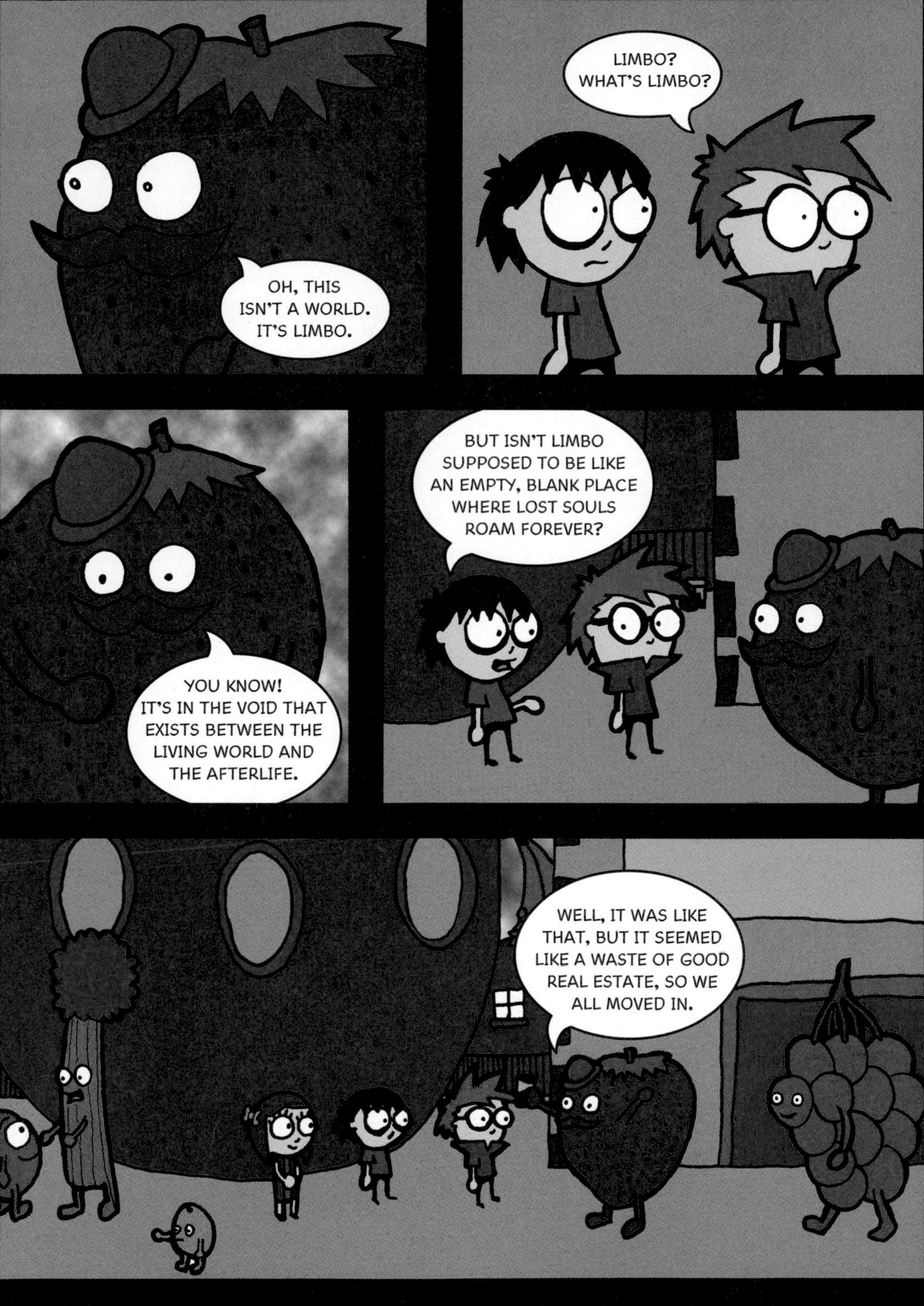
OH, THIS ISN'T A WORLD. IT'S LIMBO.
LIMBO? WHAT'S LIMBO?
YOU KNOW! IT'S IN THE VOID THAT EXISTS BETWEEN THE LIVING WORLD AND THE AFTERLIFE.
BUT ISN'T LIMBO SUPPOSED TO BE LIKE AN EMPTY, BLANK PLACE WHERE LOST SOULS ROAM FOREVER?
WELL, IT WAS LIKE THAT, BUT IT SEEMED LIKE A WASTE OF GOOD REAL ESTATE, SO WE ALL MOVED IN.

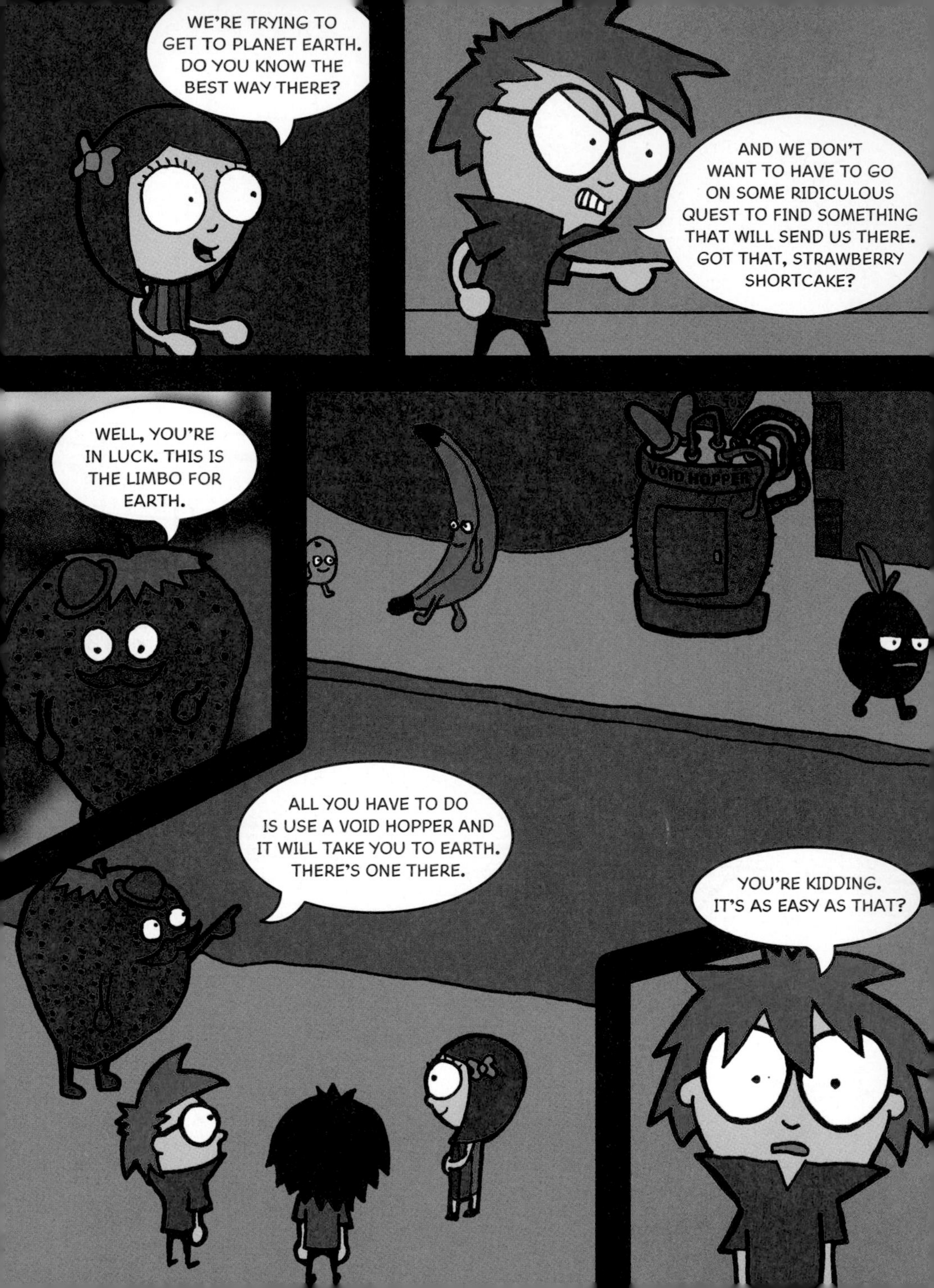
WE'RE TRYING TO GET TO PLANET EARTH. DO YOU KNOW THE BEST WAY THERE?
AND WE DON'T WANT TO HAVE TO GO ON SOME RIDICULOUS QUEST TO FIND SOMETHING THAT WILL SEND US THERE. GOT THAT, STRAWBERRY SHORTCAKE?
WELL, YOU'RE IN LUCK. THIS IS THE LIMBO FOR EARTH.
VOID HOPPER
ALL YOU HAVE TO DO IS USE A VOID HOPPER AND IT WILL TAKE YOU TO EARTH. THERE'S ONE THERE.
YOU'RE KIDDING. IT'S AS EASY AS THAT?

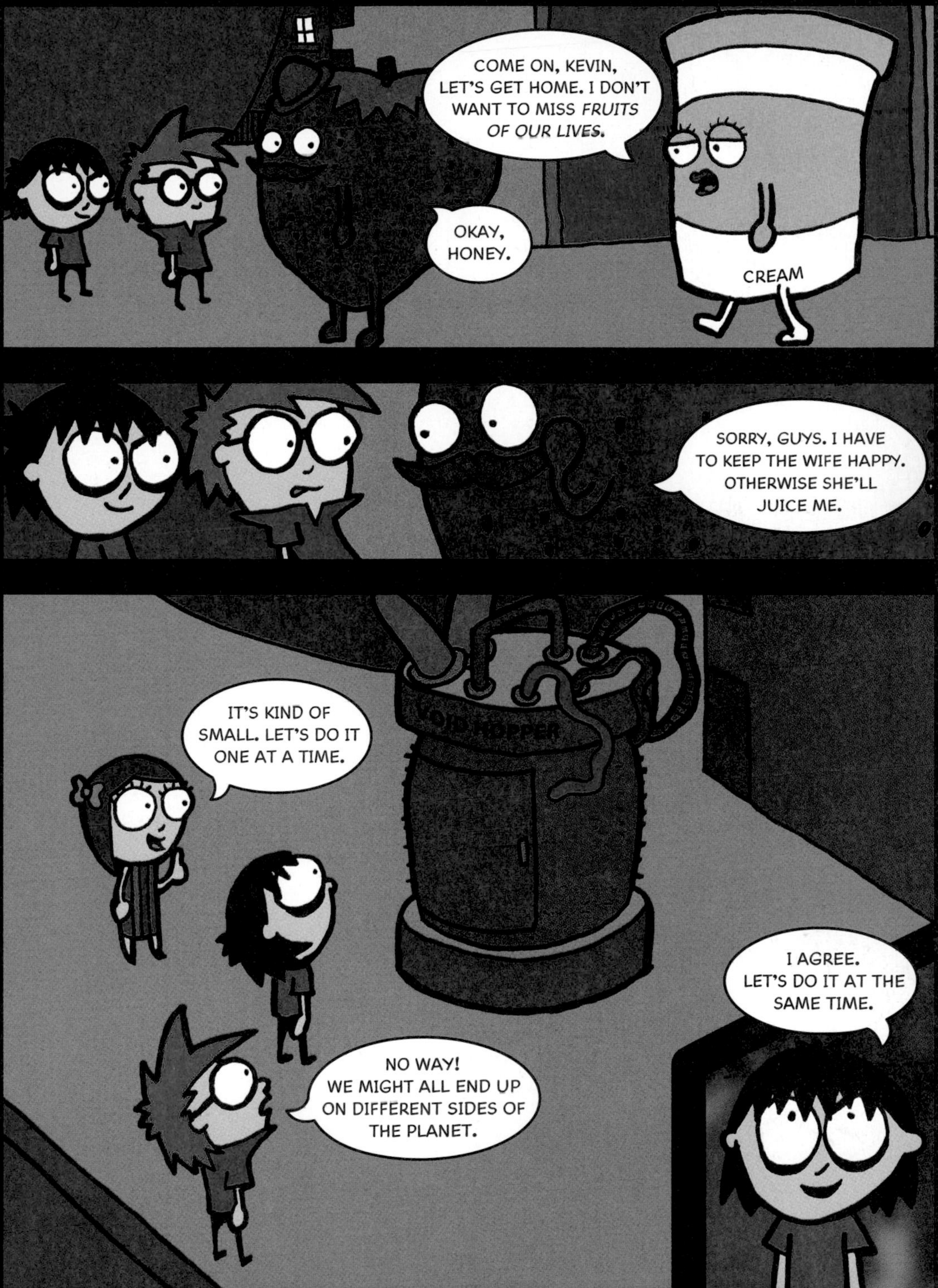
COME ON, KEVIN, LET'S GET HOME. I DON'T WANT TO MISS *FRUITS OF OUR LIVES.*
OKAY, HONEY.
CREAM
SORRY, GUYS. I HAVE TO KEEP THE WIFE HAPPY. OTHERWISE SHE'LL JUICE ME.
VOID HOPPER
IT'S KIND OF SMALL. LET'S DO IT ONE AT A TIME.
I AGREE. LET'S DO IT AT THE SAME TIME.
NO WAY! WE MIGHT ALL END UP ON DIFFERENT SIDES OF THE PLANET.

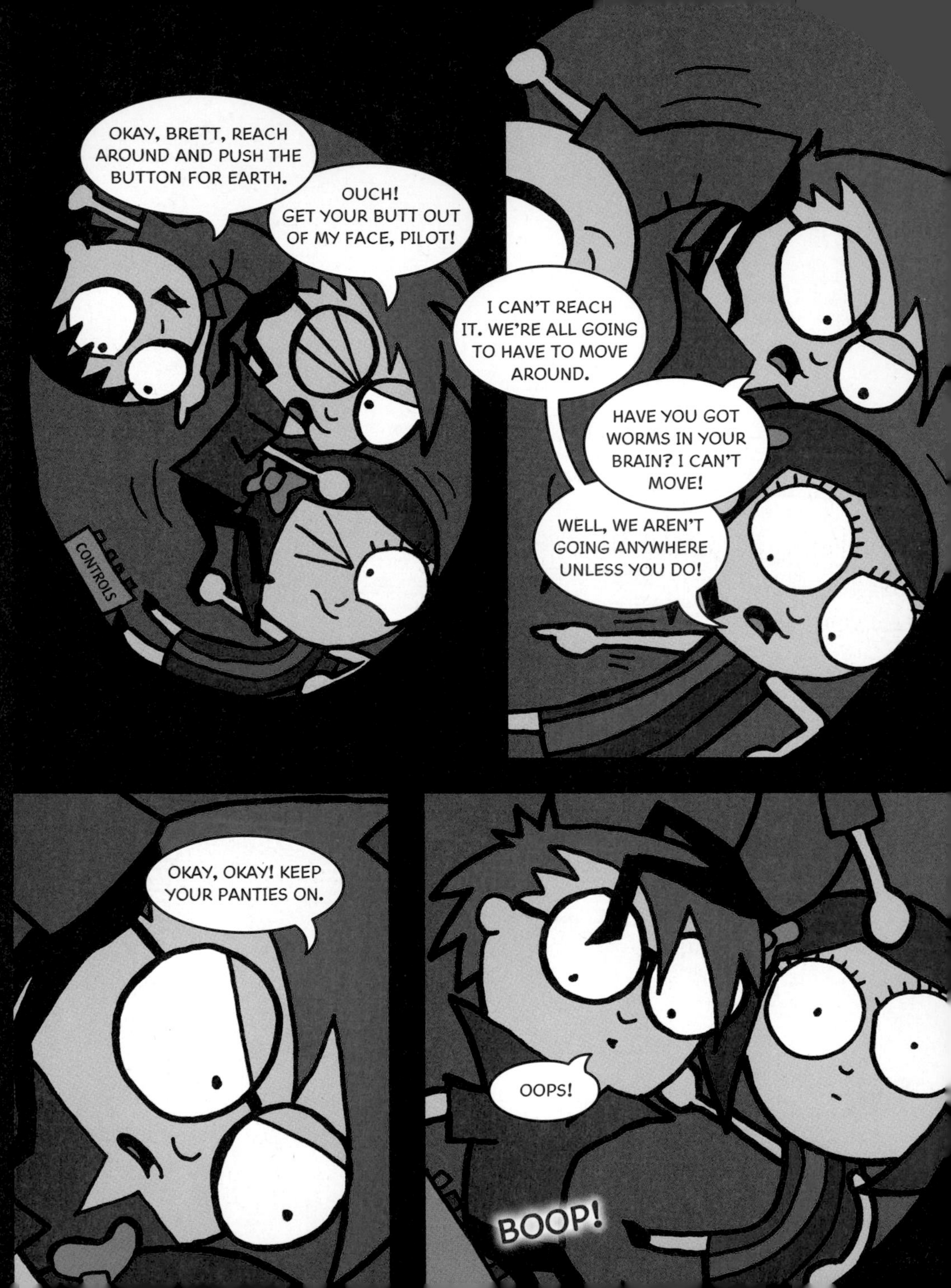
OKAY, BRETT, REACH AROUND AND PUSH THE BUTTON FOR EARTH.
OUCH! GET YOUR BUTT OUT OF MY FACE, PILOT!
CONTROLS
I CAN'T REACH IT. WE'RE ALL GOING TO HAVE TO MOVE AROUND.
HAVE YOU GOT WORMS IN YOUR BRAIN? I CAN'T MOVE!
WELL, WE AREN'T GOING ANYWHERE UNLESS YOU DO!
OKAY, OKAY! KEEP YOUR PANTIES ON.
OOPS!
BOOP!

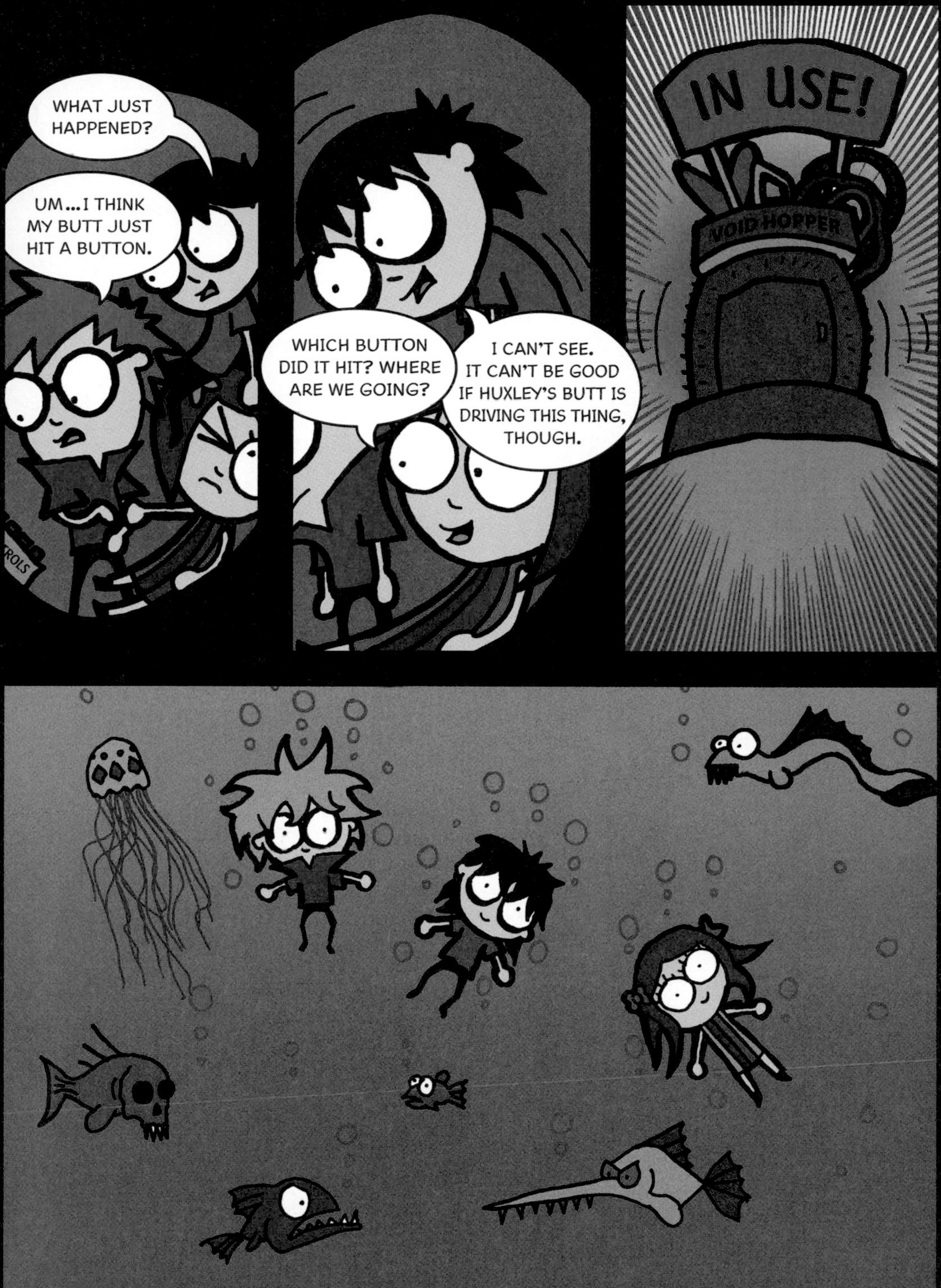
WHAT JUST HAPPENED?
UM...I THINK MY BUTT JUST HIT A BUTTON.
WHICH BUTTON DID IT HIT? WHERE ARE WE GOING?
I CAN'T SEE. IT CAN'T BE GOOD IF HUXLEY'S BUTT IS DRIVING THIS THING, THOUGH.
IN USE!
VOID HOPPER

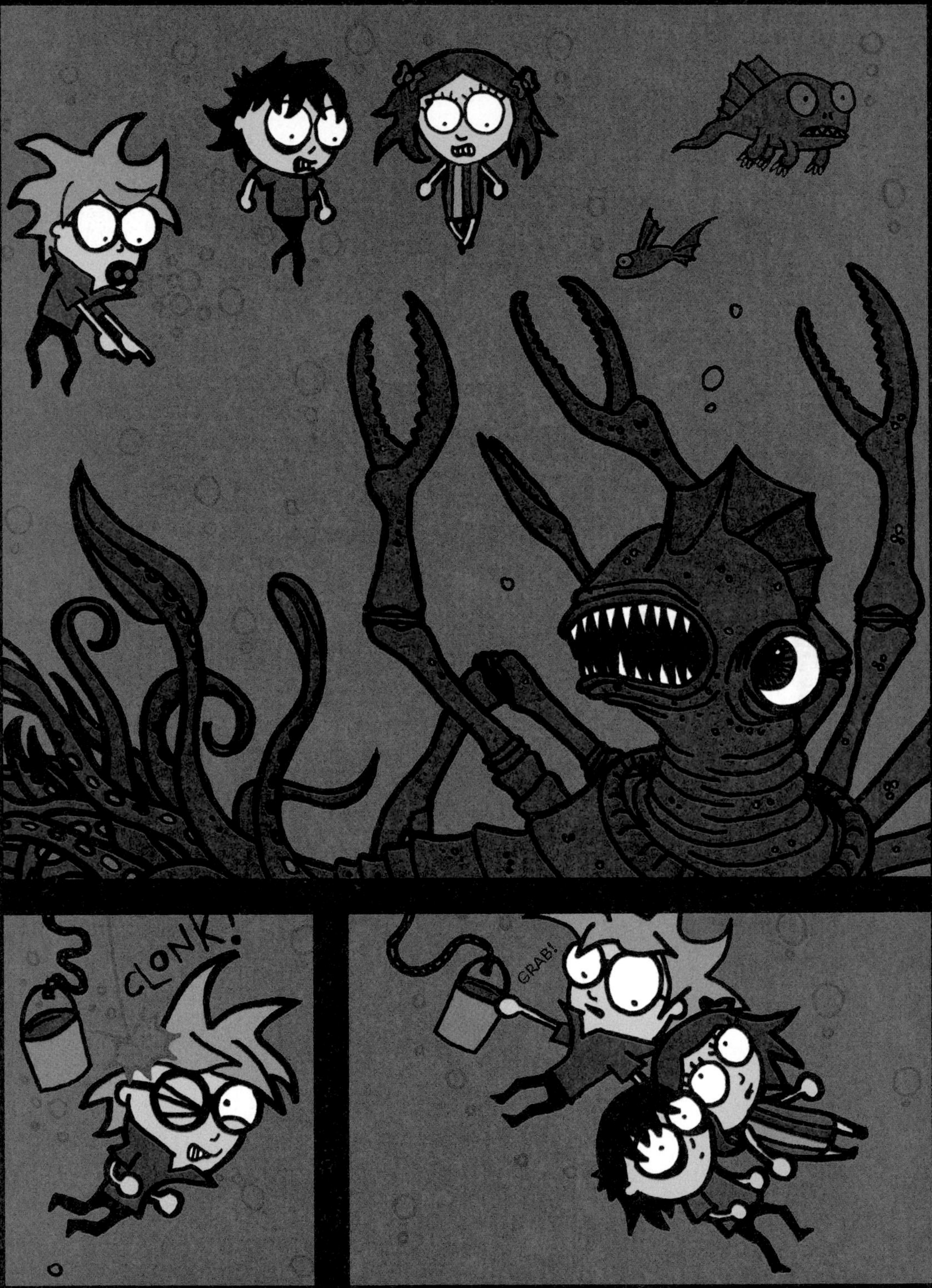
CLONK!
GRAB!

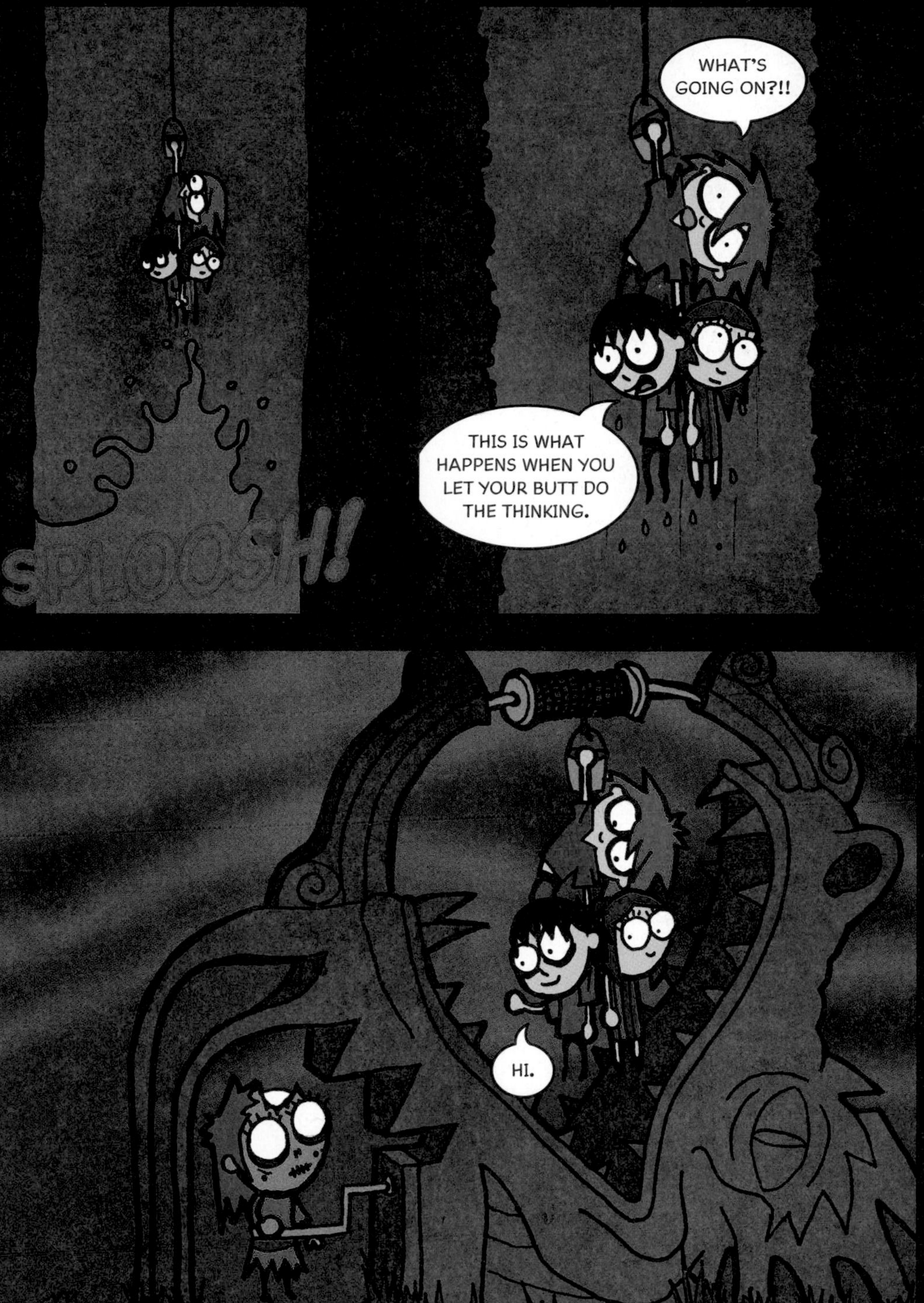
SPLOOSH!
WHAT'S GOING ON?!!
THIS IS WHAT HAPPENS WHEN YOU LET YOUR BUTT DO THE THINKING.
HI.

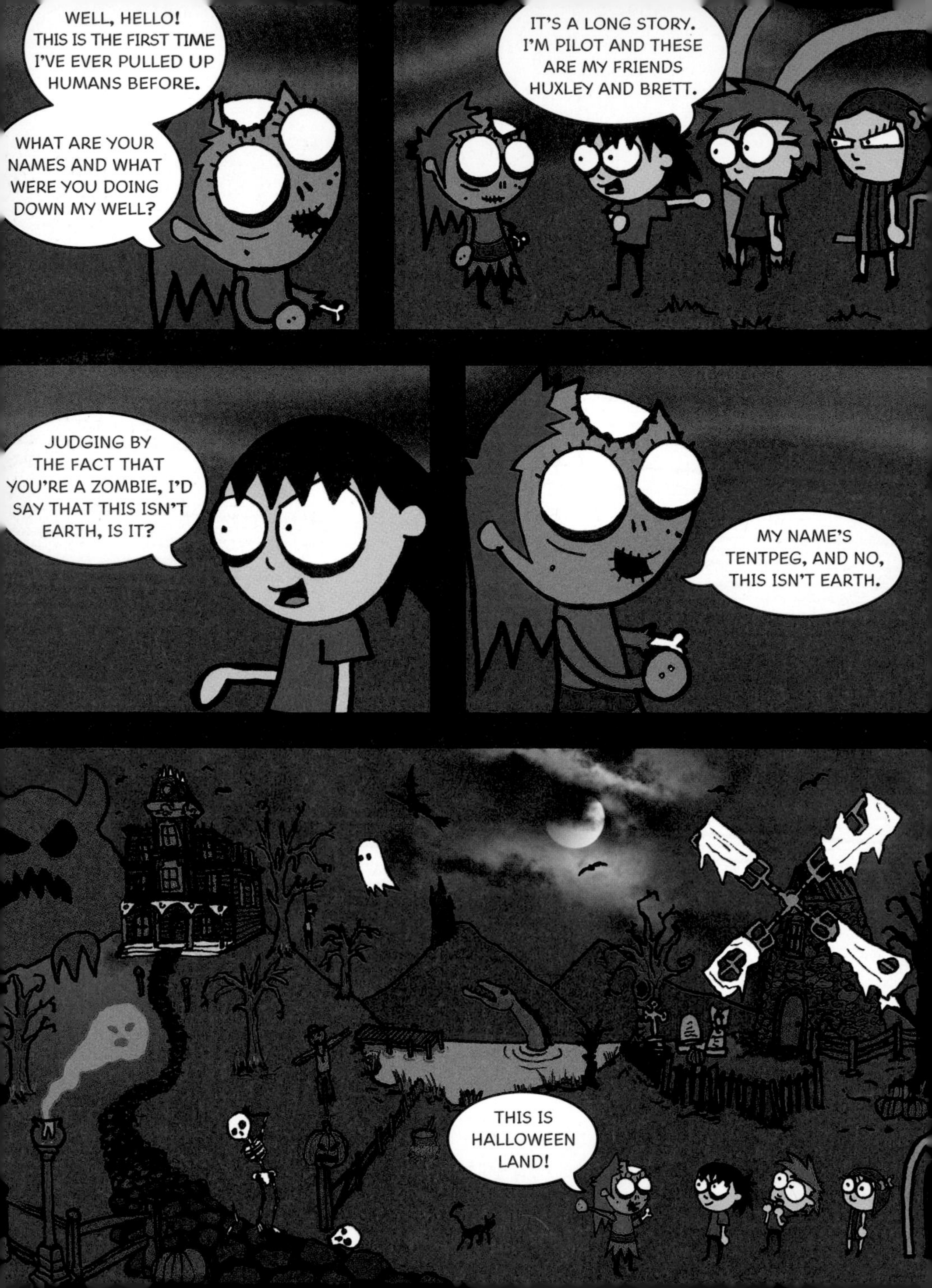

WELL, HELLO! THIS IS THE FIRST TIME I'VE EVER PULLED UP HUMANS BEFORE.
WHAT ARE YOUR NAMES AND WHAT WERE YOU DOING DOWN MY WELL?
IT'S A LONG STORY. I'M PILOT AND THESE ARE MY FRIENDS HUXLEY AND BRETT.
JUDGING BY THE FACT THAT YOU'RE A ZOMBIE, I'D SAY THAT THIS ISN'T EARTH, IS IT?
MY NAME'S TENTPEG, AND NO, THIS ISN'T EARTH.
THIS IS HALLOWEEN LAND!

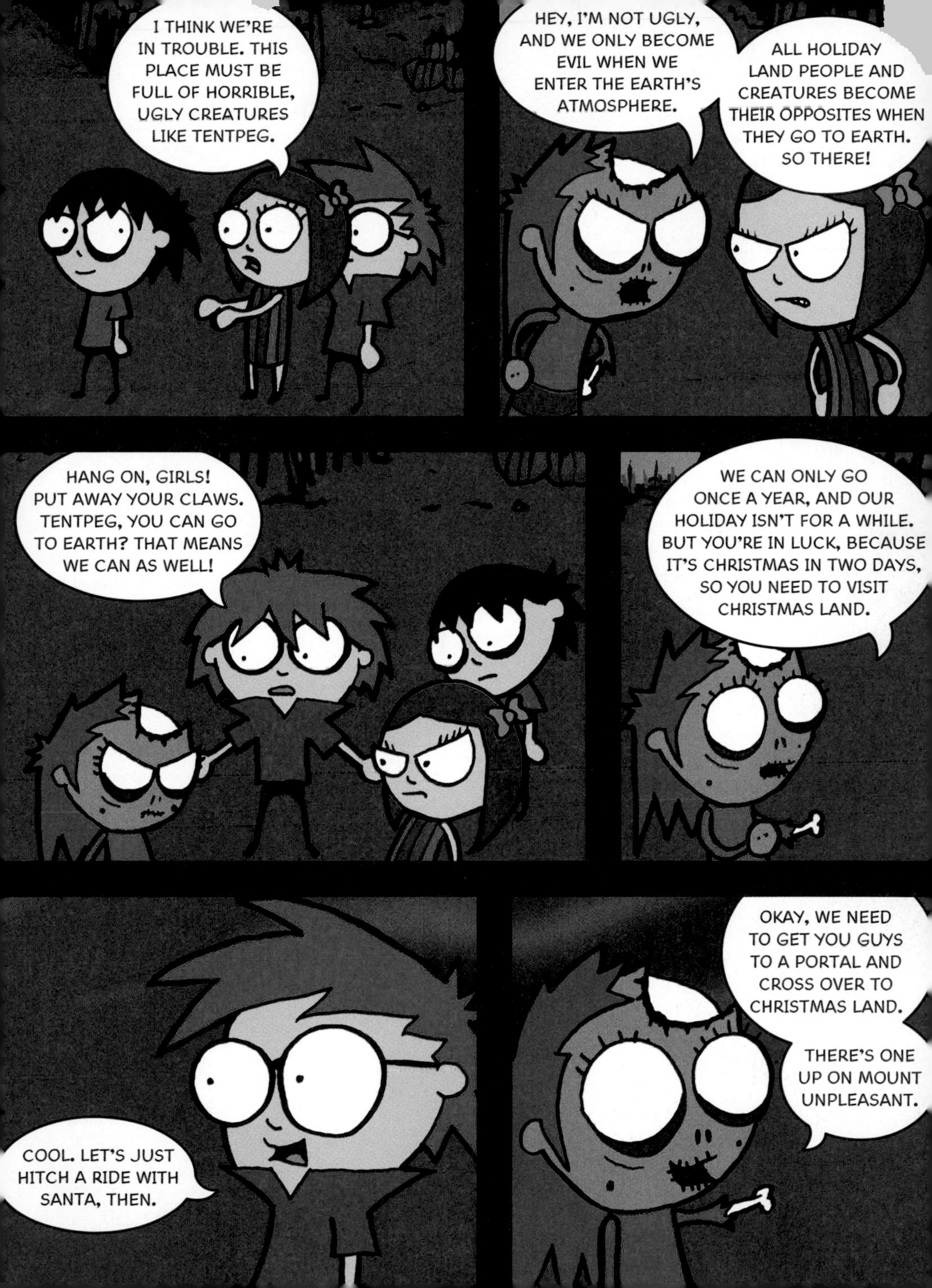
I THINK WE'RE IN TROUBLE. THIS PLACE MUST BE FULL OF HORRIBLE, UGLY CREATURES LIKE TENTPEG.
HEY, I'M NOT UGLY, AND WE ONLY BECOME EVIL WHEN WE ENTER THE EARTH'S ATMOSPHERE.
ALL HOLIDAY LAND PEOPLE AND CREATURES BECOME THEIR OPPOSITES WHEN THEY GO TO EARTH. SO THERE!
HANG ON, GIRLS! PUT AWAY YOUR CLAWS. TENTPEG, YOU CAN GO TO EARTH? THAT MEANS WE CAN AS WELL!
WE CAN ONLY GO ONCE A YEAR, AND OUR HOLIDAY ISN'T FOR A WHILE. BUT YOU'RE IN LUCK, BECAUSE IT'S CHRISTMAS IN TWO DAYS, SO YOU NEED TO VISIT CHRISTMAS LAND.
COOL. LET'S JUST HITCH A RIDE WITH SANTA, THEN.
OKAY, WE NEED TO GET YOU GUYS TO A PORTAL AND CROSS OVER TO CHRISTMAS LAND.
THERE'S ONE UP ON MOUNT UNPLEASANT.

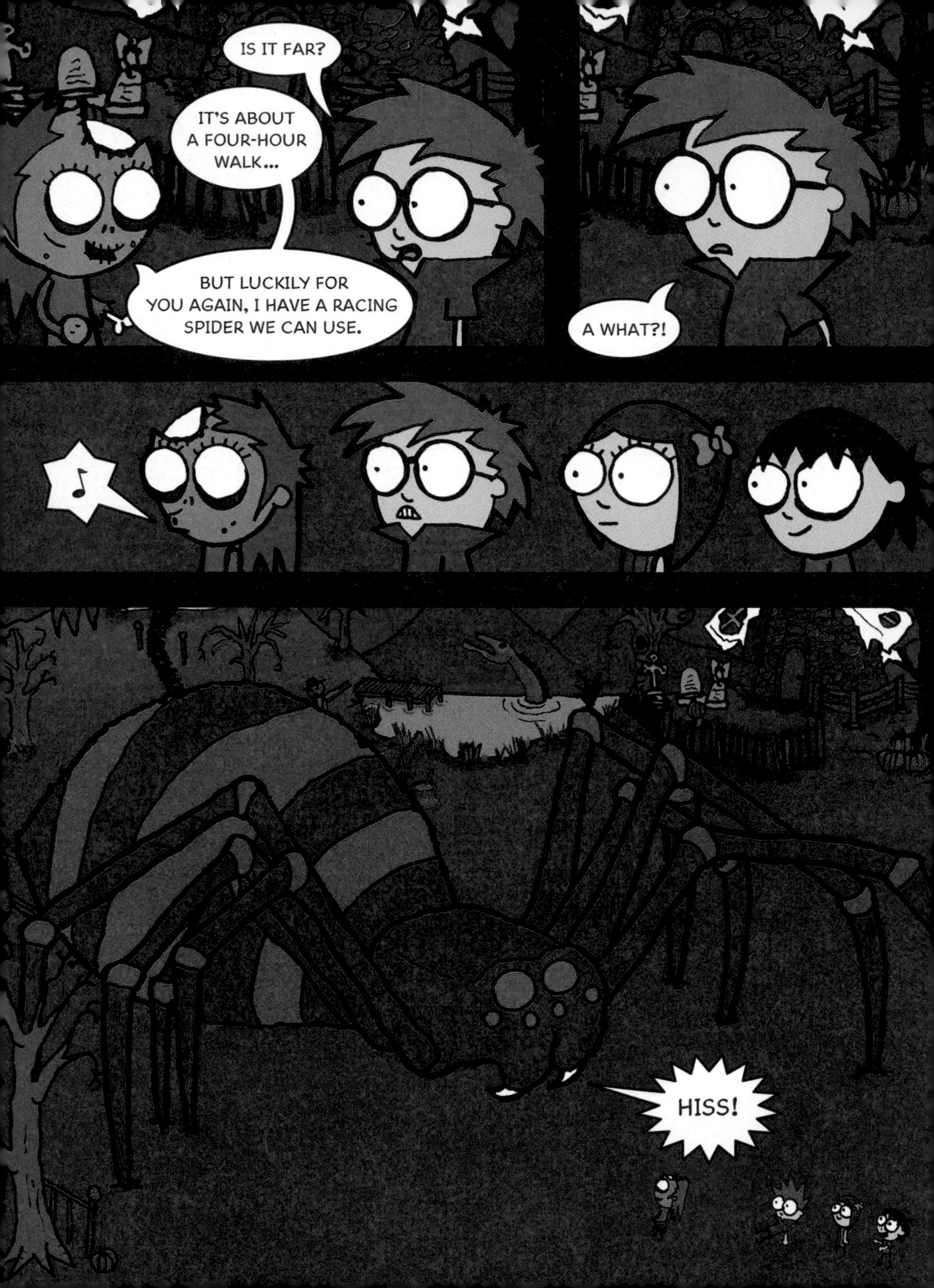
IS IT FAR?
IT'S ABOUT A FOUR-HOUR WALK...
BUT LUCKILY FOR YOU AGAIN, I HAVE A RACING SPIDER WE CAN USE.
A WHAT?!
♪
HISS!

CHAPTER TWO

DECK THE HALLS...

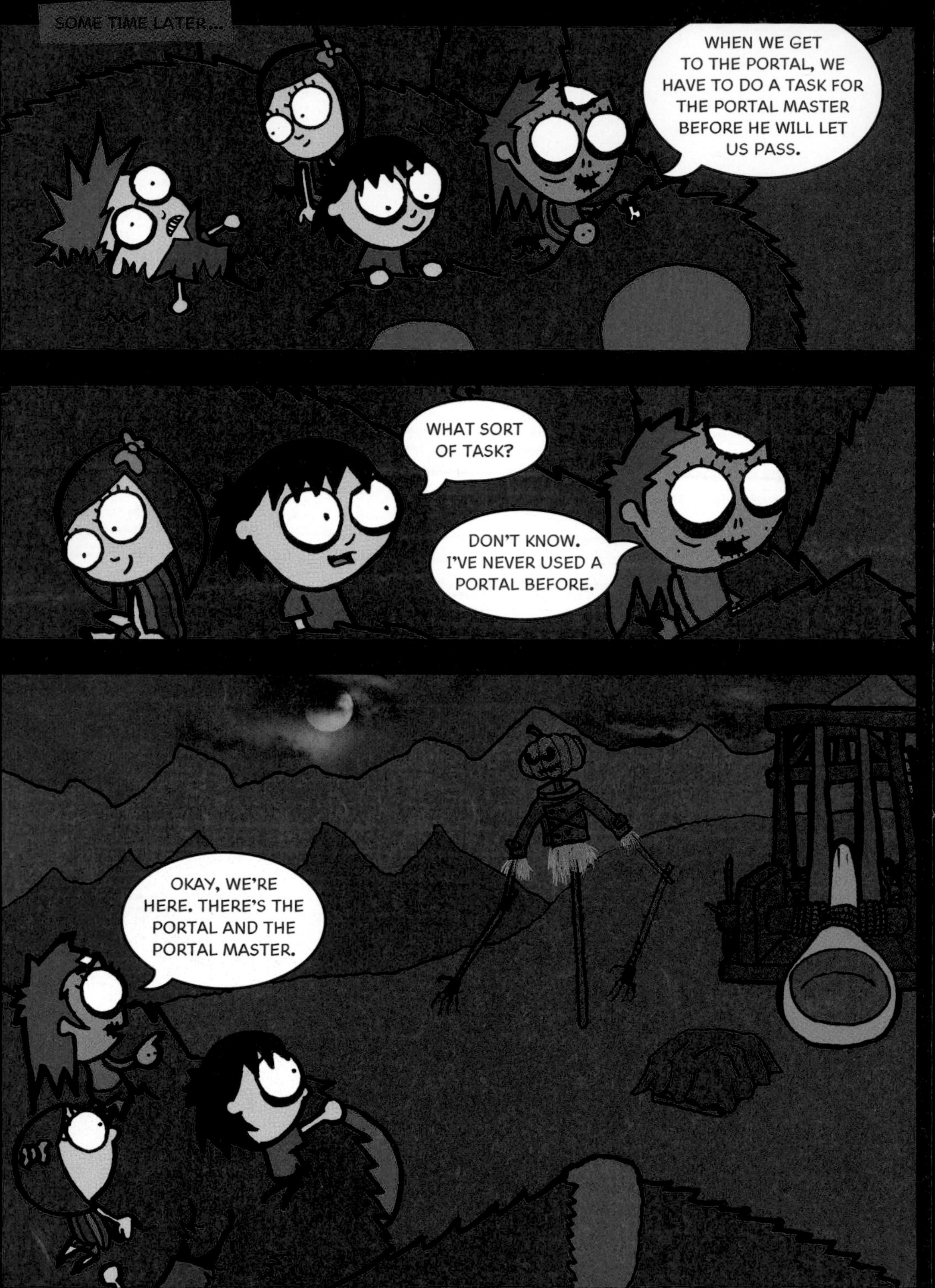
SOME TIME LATER...
WHEN WE GET TO THE PORTAL, WE HAVE TO DO A TASK FOR THE PORTAL MASTER BEFORE HE WILL LET US PASS.
WHAT SORT OF TASK?
DON'T KNOW. I'VE NEVER USED A PORTAL BEFORE.
OKAY, WE'RE HERE. THERE'S THE PORTAL AND THE PORTAL MASTER.

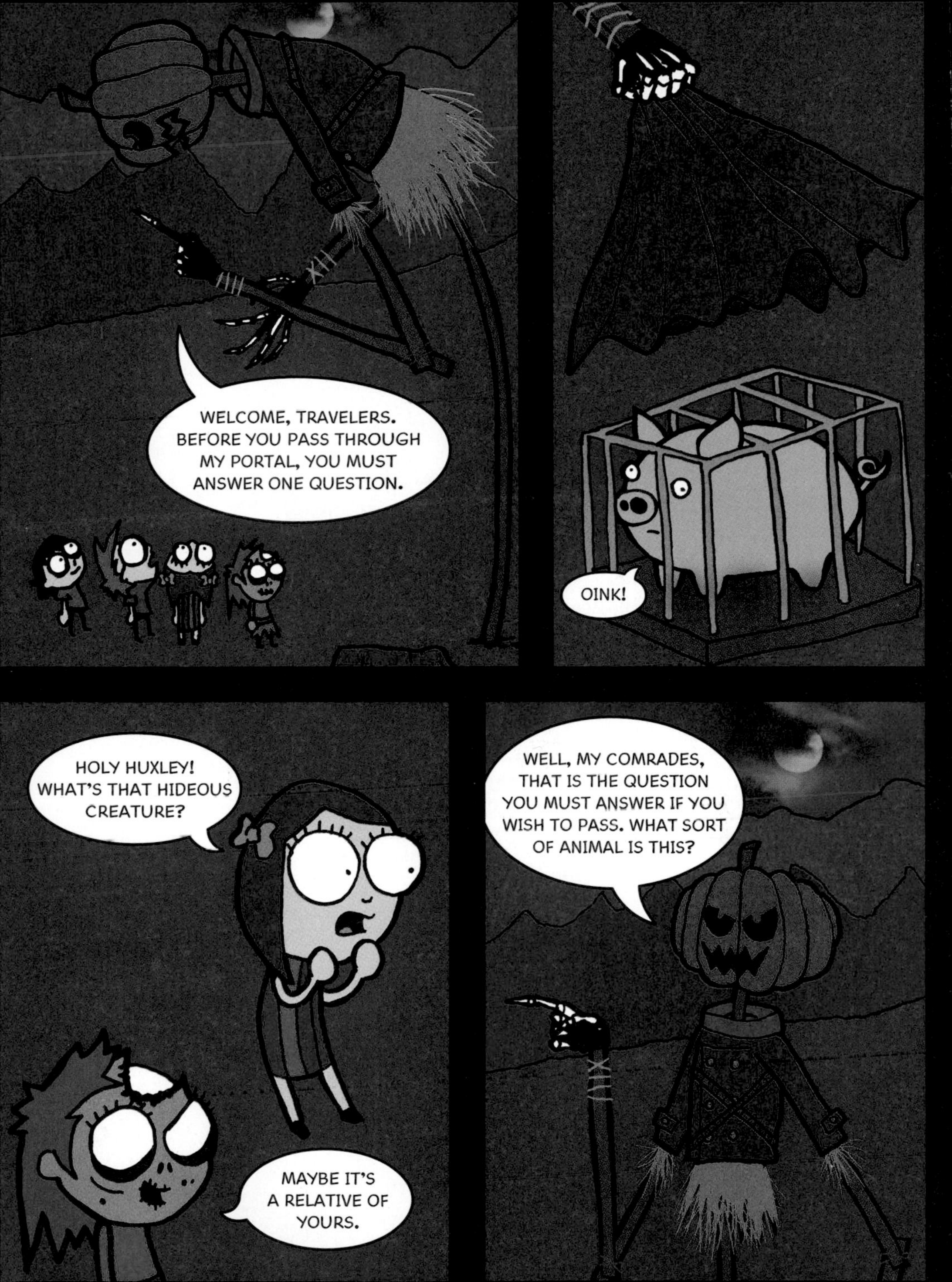
WELCOME, TRAVELERS. BEFORE YOU PASS THROUGH MY PORTAL, YOU MUST ANSWER ONE QUESTION.
OINK!
HOLY HUXLEY! WHAT'S THAT HIDEOUS CREATURE?
MAYBE IT'S A RELATIVE OF YOURS.
WELL, MY COMRADES, THAT IS THE QUESTION YOU MUST ANSWER IF YOU WISH TO PASS. WHAT SORT OF ANIMAL IS THIS?

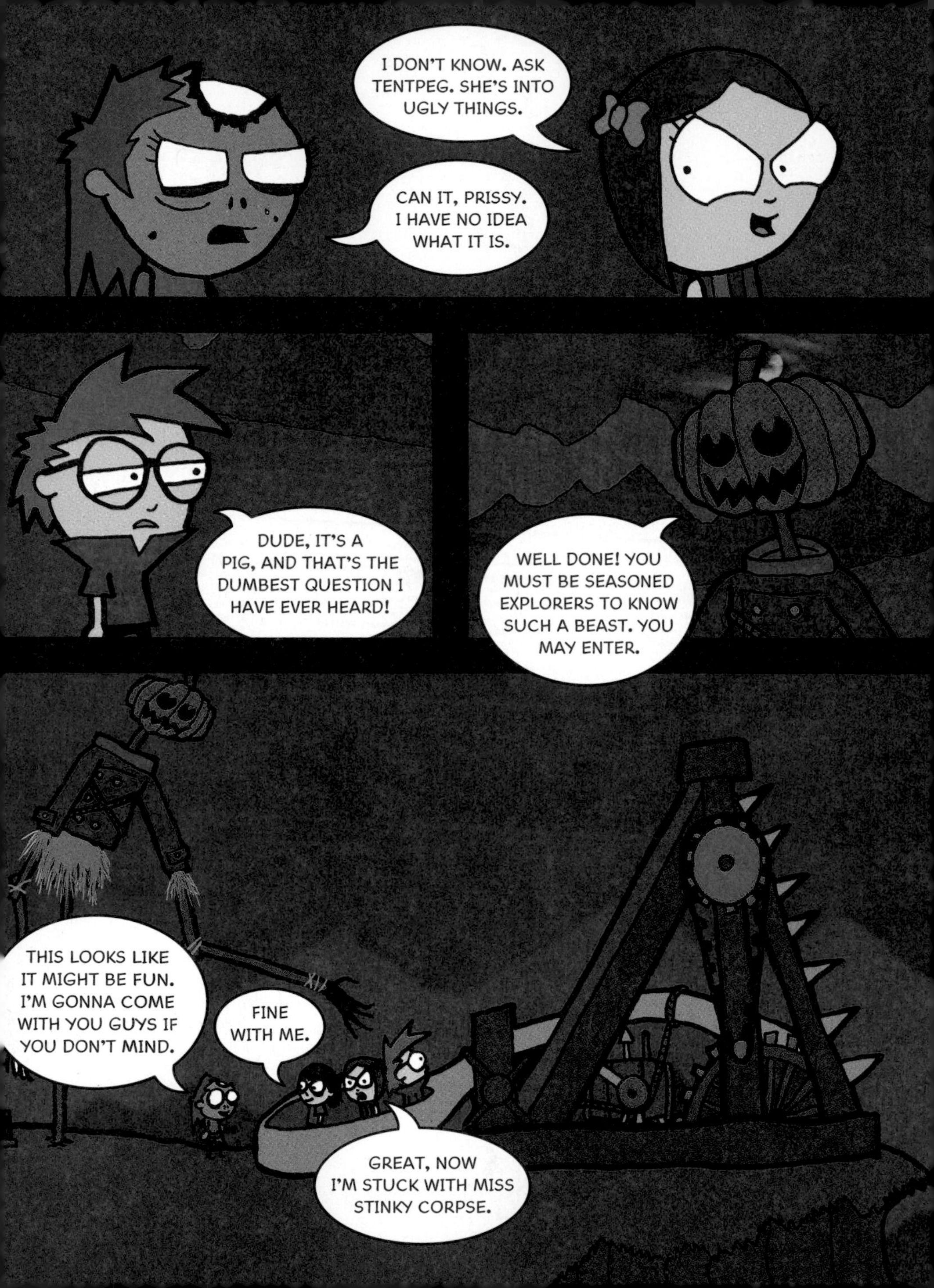
I DON'T KNOW. ASK TENTPEG. SHE'S INTO UGLY THINGS.
CAN IT, PRISSY. I HAVE NO IDEA WHAT IT IS.
DUDE, IT'S A PIG, AND THAT'S THE DUMBEST QUESTION I HAVE EVER HEARD!
WELL DONE! YOU MUST BE SEASONED EXPLORERS TO KNOW SUCH A BEAST. YOU MAY ENTER.
THIS LOOKS LIKE IT MIGHT BE FUN. I'M GONNA COME WITH YOU GUYS IF YOU DON'T MIND.
FINE WITH ME.
GREAT, NOW I'M STUCK WITH MISS STINKY CORPSE.

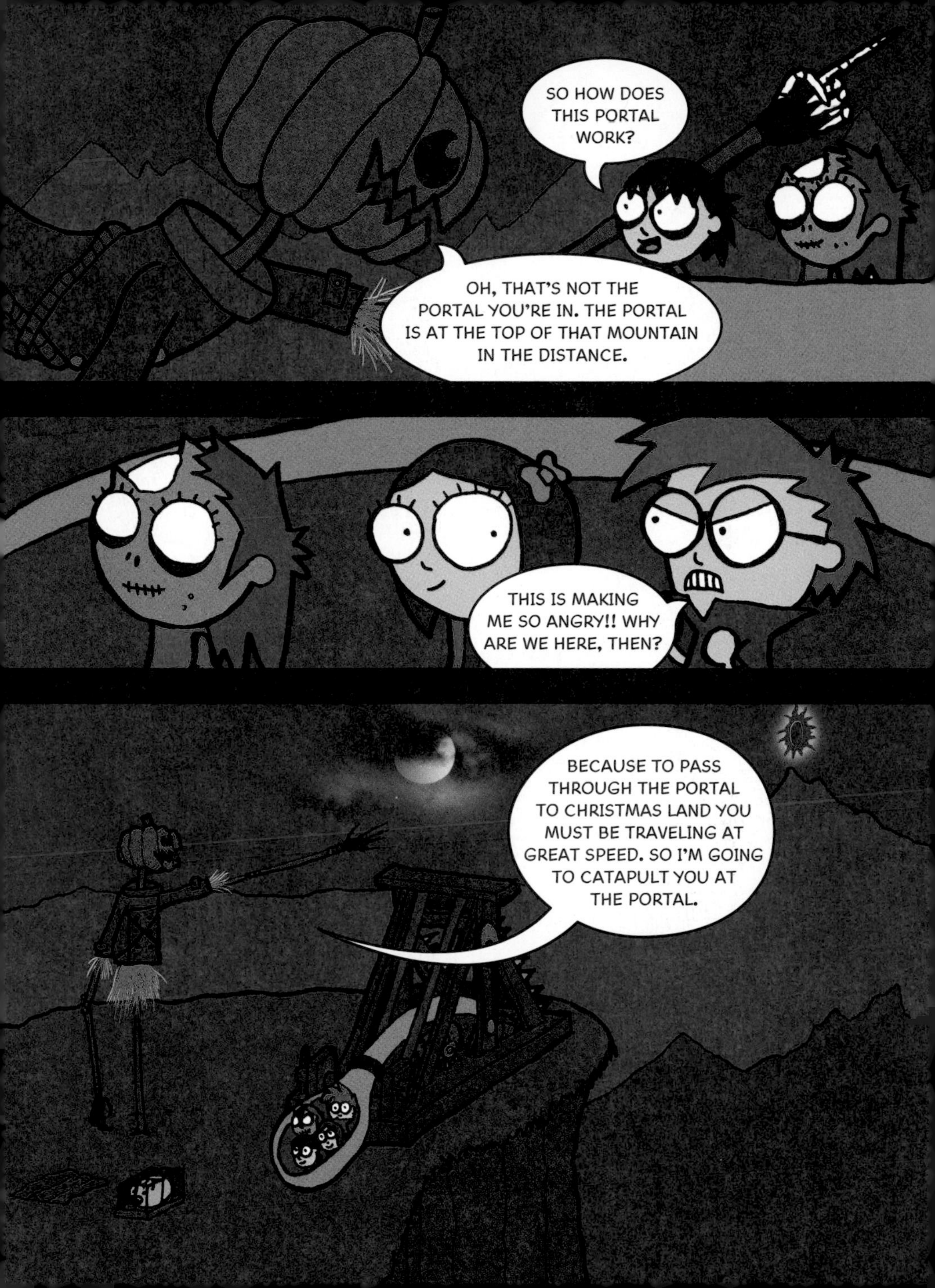
SO HOW DOES THIS PORTAL WORK?
OH, THAT'S NOT THE PORTAL YOU'RE IN. THE PORTAL IS AT THE TOP OF THAT MOUNTAIN IN THE DISTANCE.
THIS IS MAKING ME SO ANGRY!! WHY ARE WE HERE, THEN?
BECAUSE TO PASS THROUGH THE PORTAL TO CHRISTMAS LAND YOU MUST BE TRAVELING AT GREAT SPEED. SO I'M GOING TO CATAPULT YOU AT THE PORTAL.

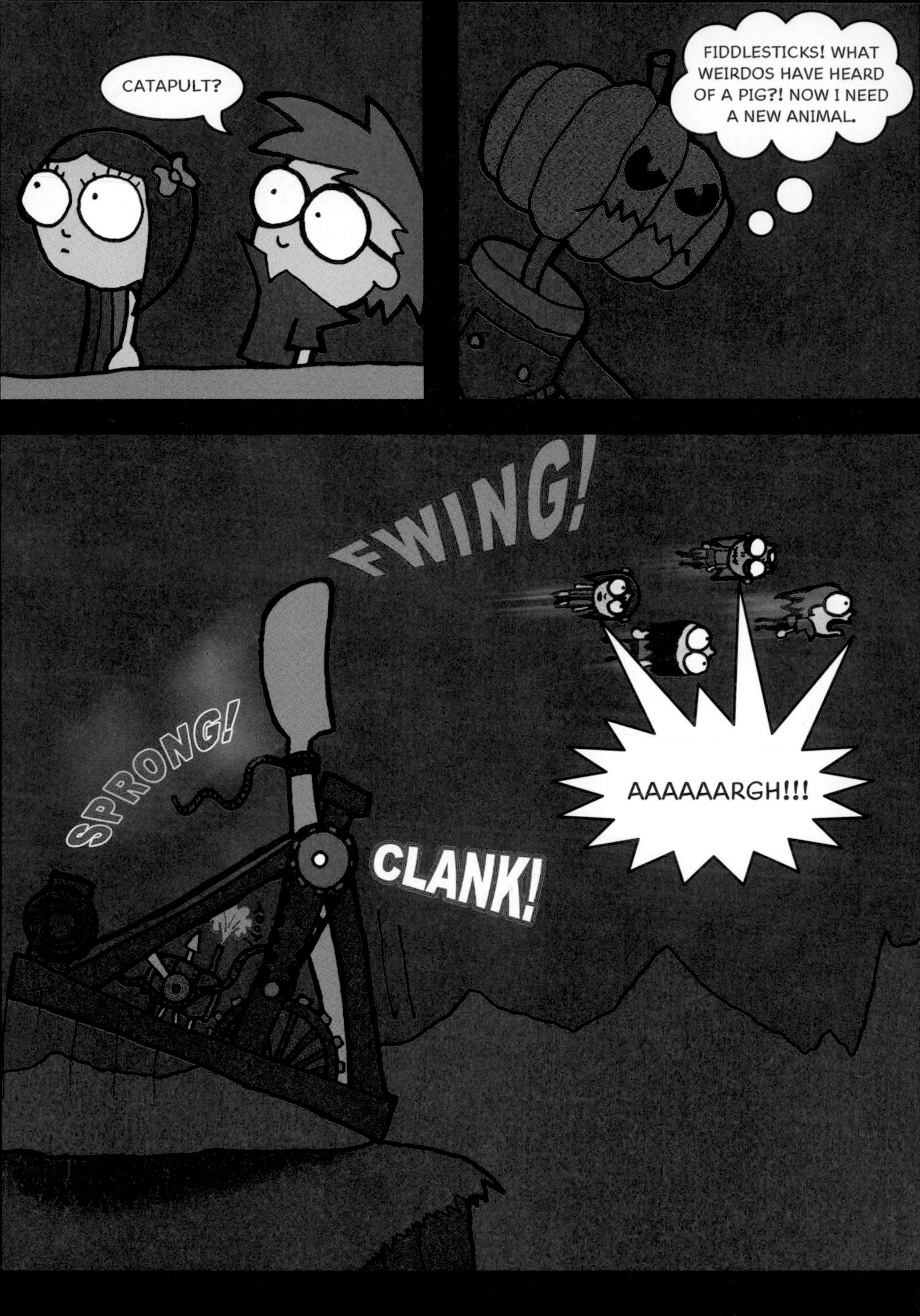
CATAPULT?
FIDDLESTICKS! WHAT WEIRDOS HAVE HEARD OF A PIG?! NOW I NEED A NEW ANIMAL.
FWING!
SPRONG!
CLANK!
AAAAAARGH!!!

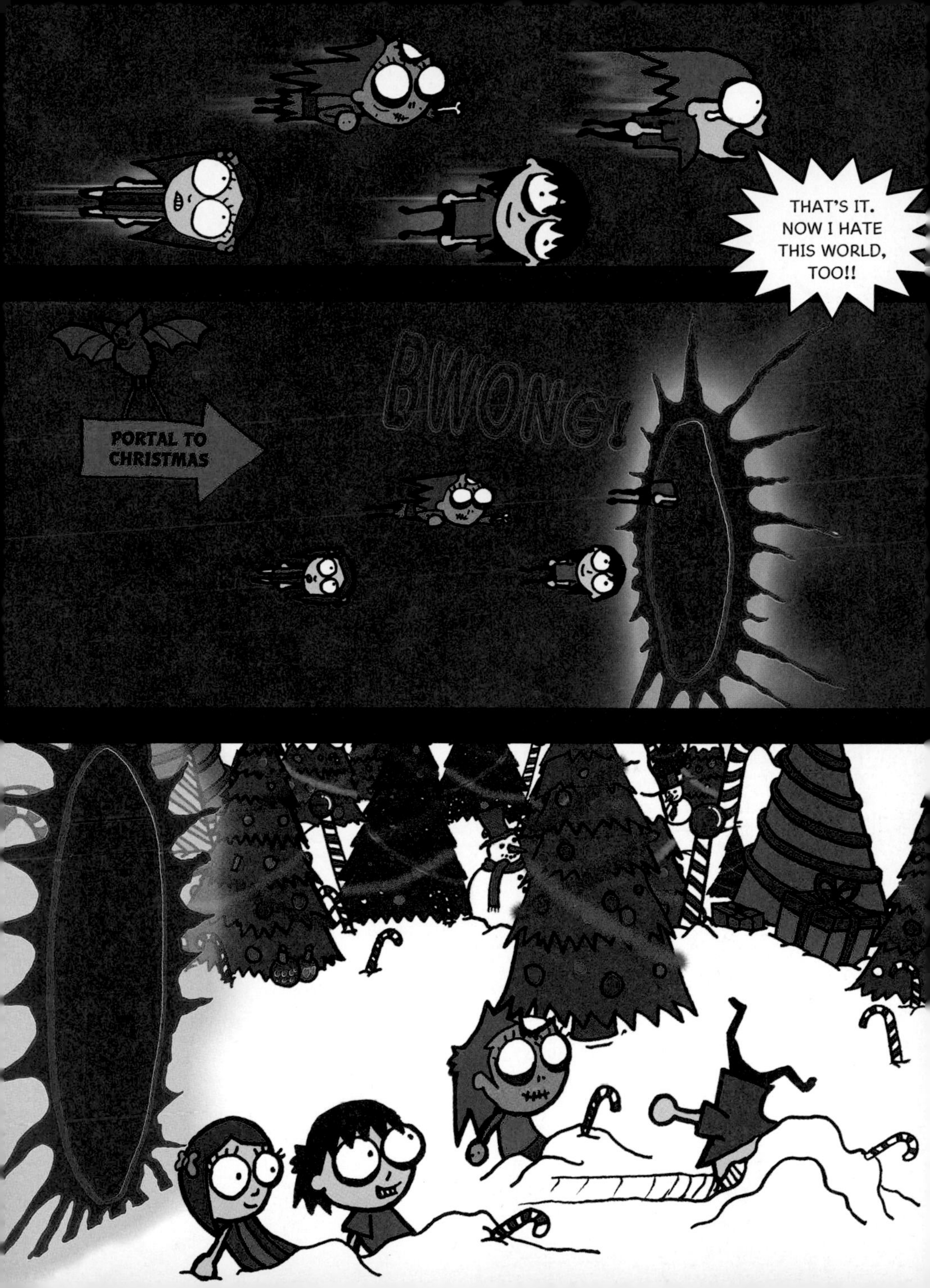
THAT'S IT. NOW I HATE THIS WORLD, TOO!!
PORTAL TO CHRISTMAS
BWONG!

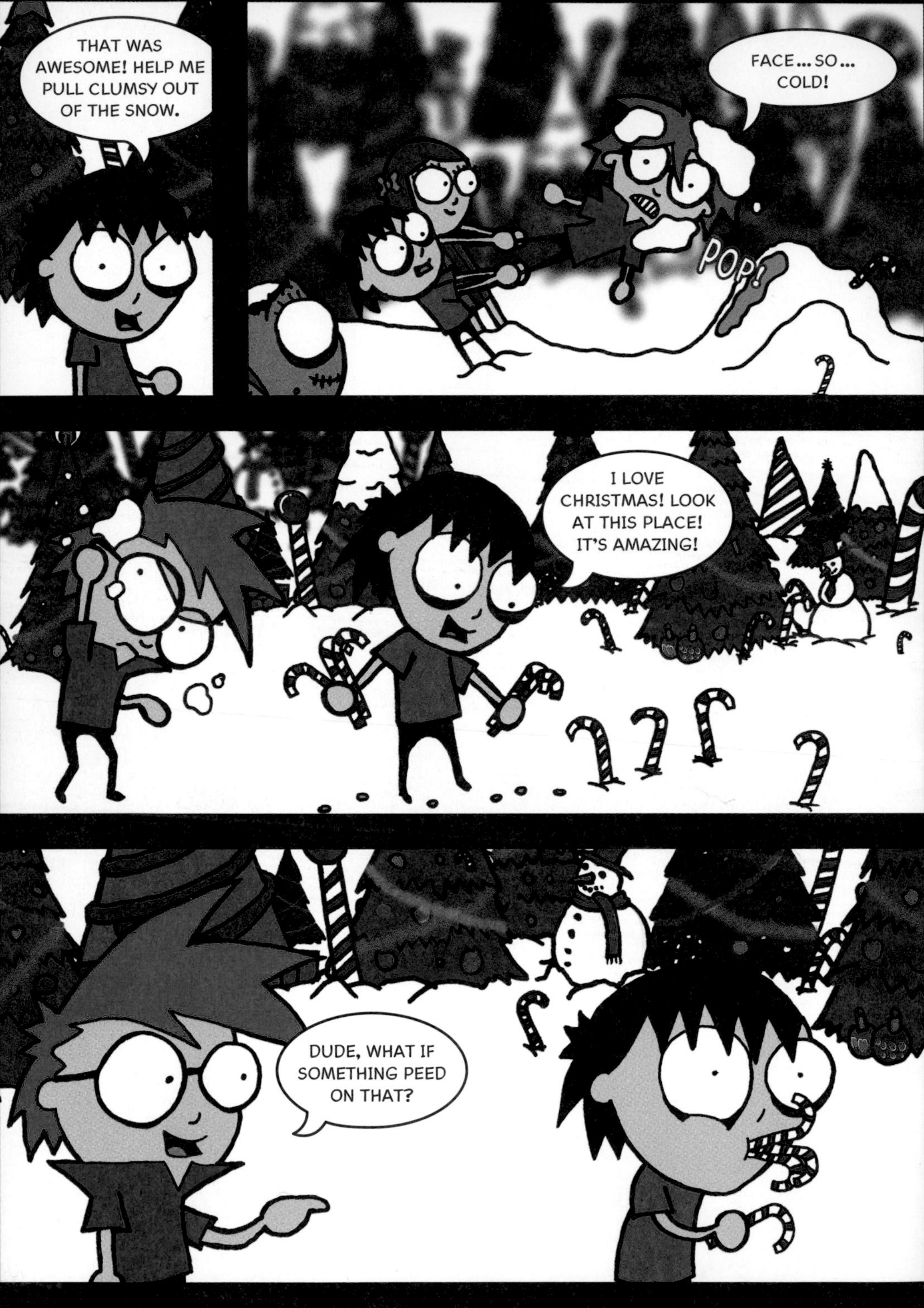
THAT WAS AWESOME! HELP ME PULL CLUMSY OUT OF THE SNOW.
FACE... SO... COLD!
POP!
I LOVE CHRISTMAS! LOOK AT THIS PLACE! IT'S AMAZING!
DUDE, WHAT IF SOMETHING PEED ON THAT?

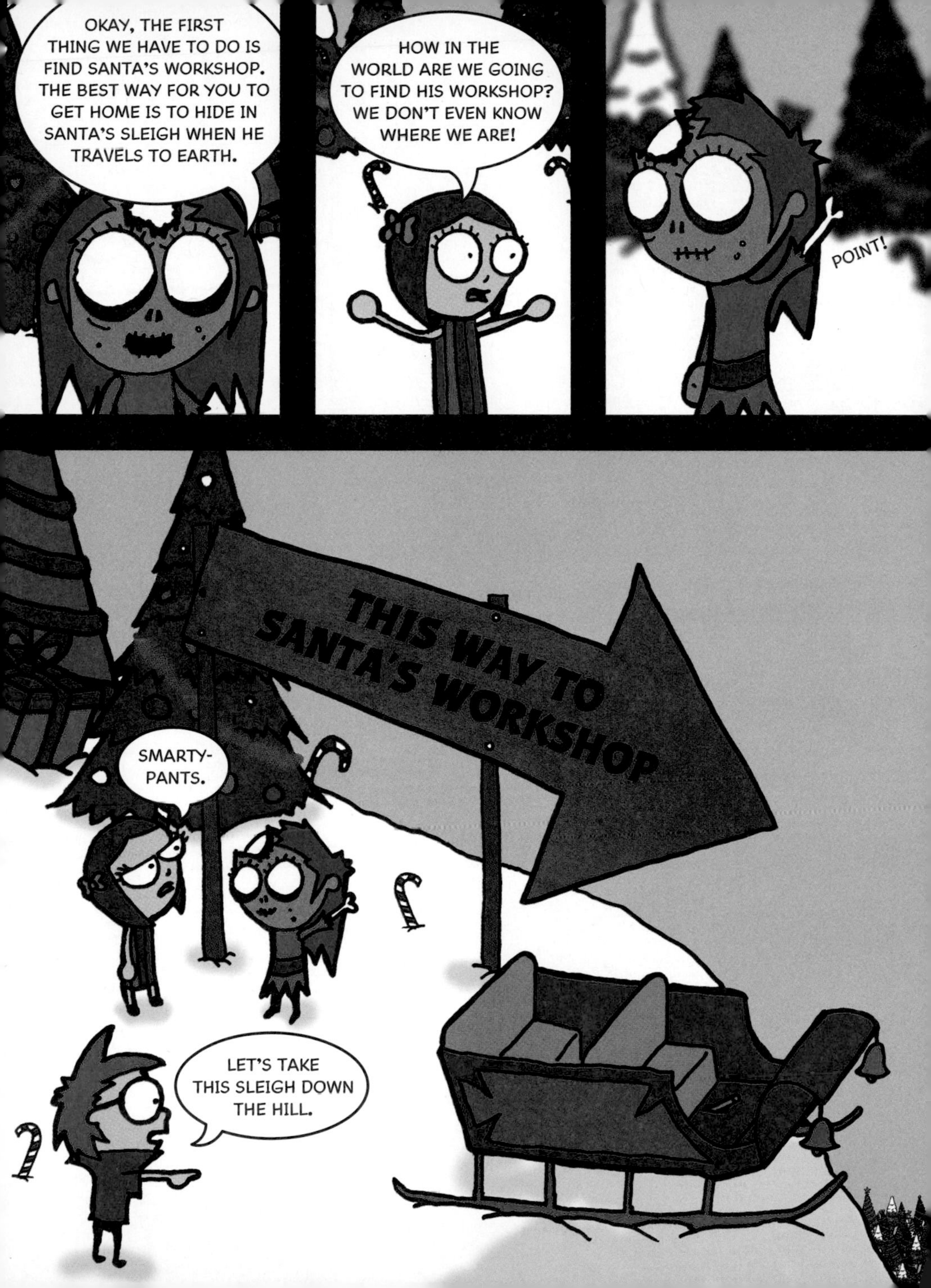
OKAY, THE FIRST THING WE HAVE TO DO IS FIND SANTA'S WORKSHOP. THE BEST WAY FOR YOU TO GET HOME IS TO HIDE IN SANTA'S SLEIGH WHEN HE TRAVELS TO EARTH.
HOW IN THE WORLD ARE WE GOING TO FIND HIS WORKSHOP? WE DON'T EVEN KNOW WHERE WE ARE!
POINT!
THIS WAY TO SANTA'S WORKSHOP
SMARTY-PANTS.
LET'S TAKE THIS SLEIGH DOWN THE HILL.

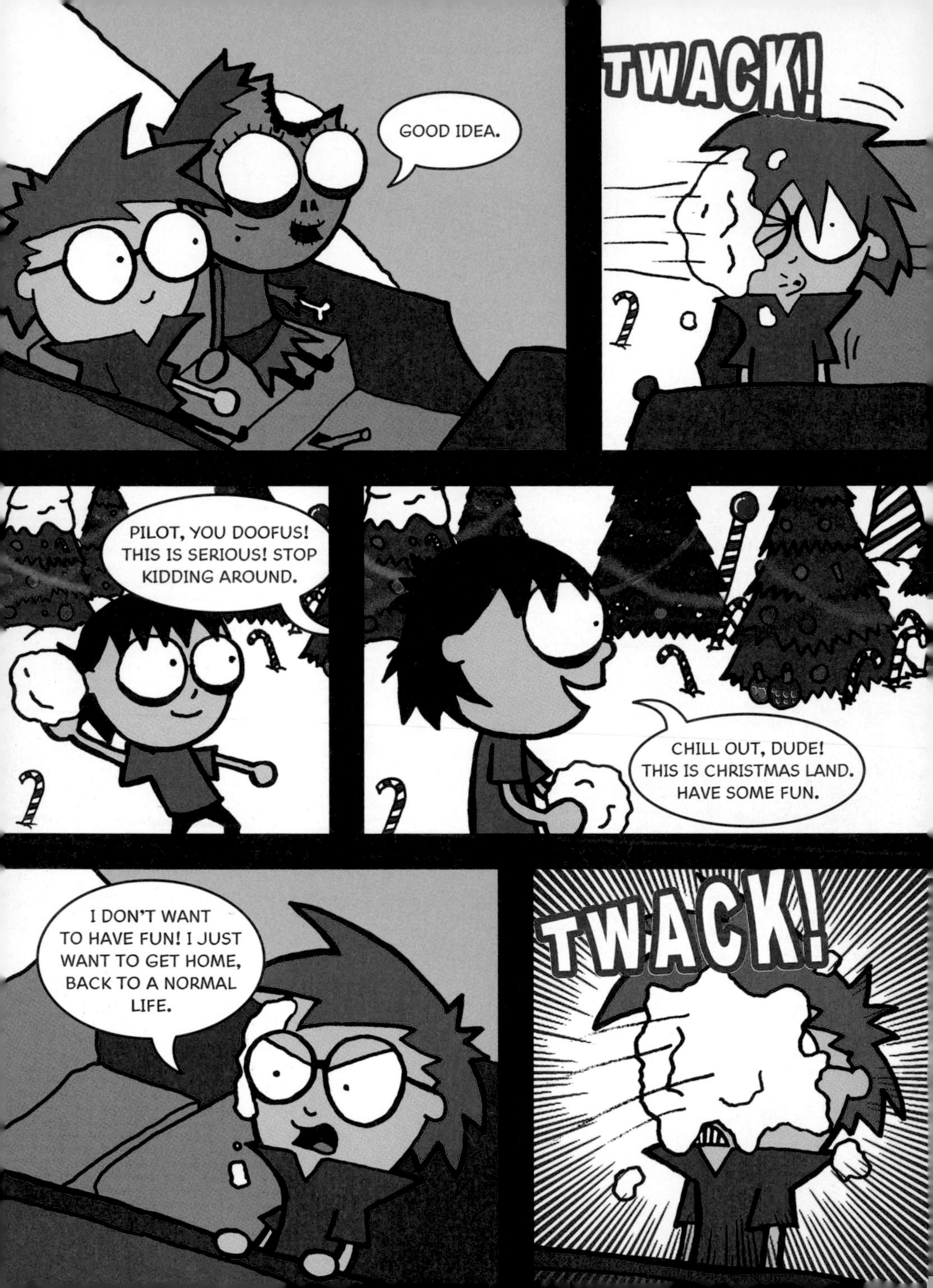
GOOD IDEA.
TWACK!
PILOT, YOU DOOFUS! THIS IS SERIOUS! STOP KIDDING AROUND.
CHILL OUT, DUDE! THIS IS CHRISTMAS LAND. HAVE SOME FUN.
I DON'T WANT TO HAVE FUN! I JUST WANT TO GET HOME, BACK TO A NORMAL LIFE.
TWACK!

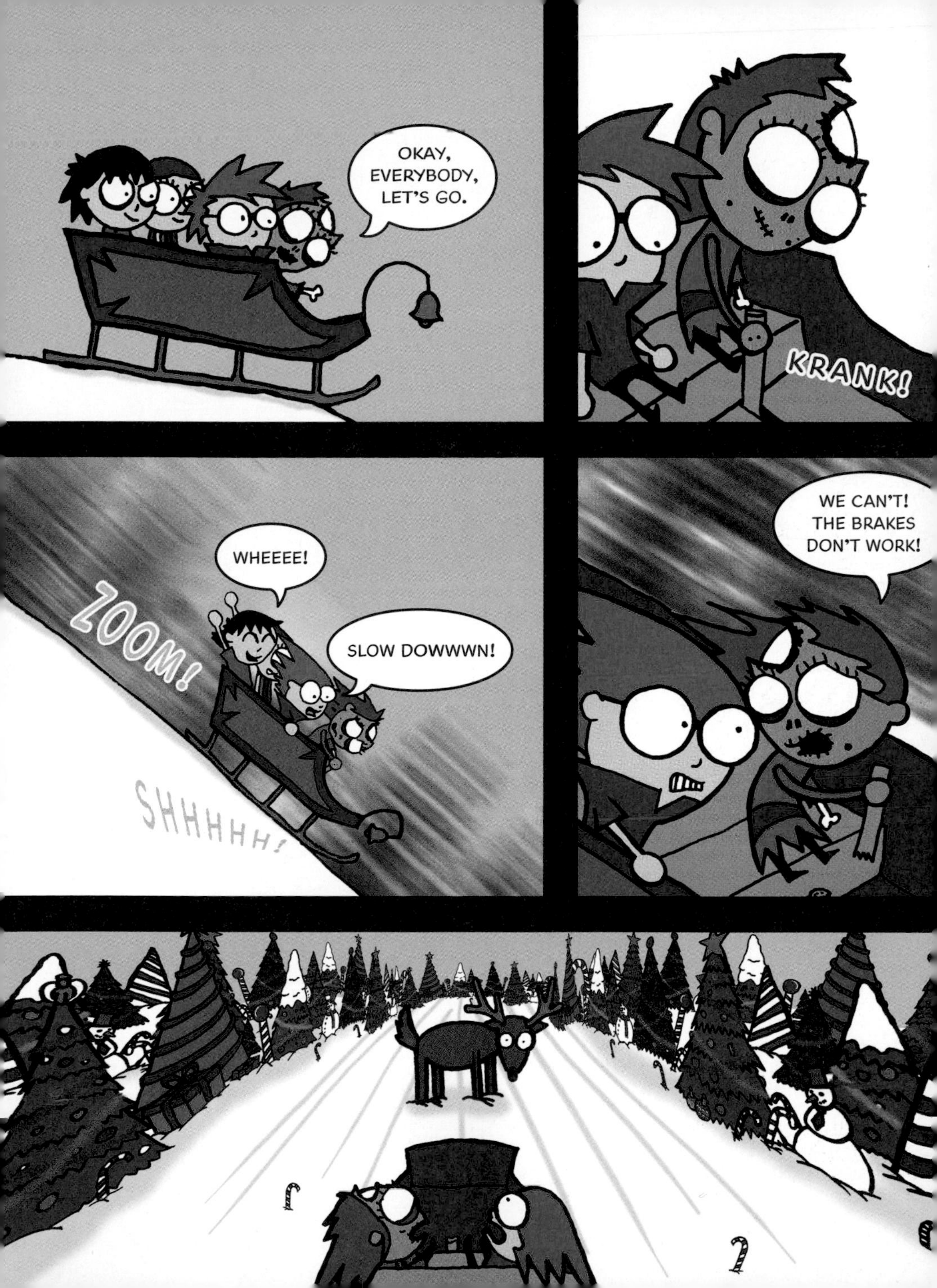
OKAY, EVERYBODY, LET'S GO.
KRANK!
WHEEEE!
ZOOM!
SLOW DOWWWN!
SHHHHHH!
WE CAN'T! THE BRAKES DON'T WORK!

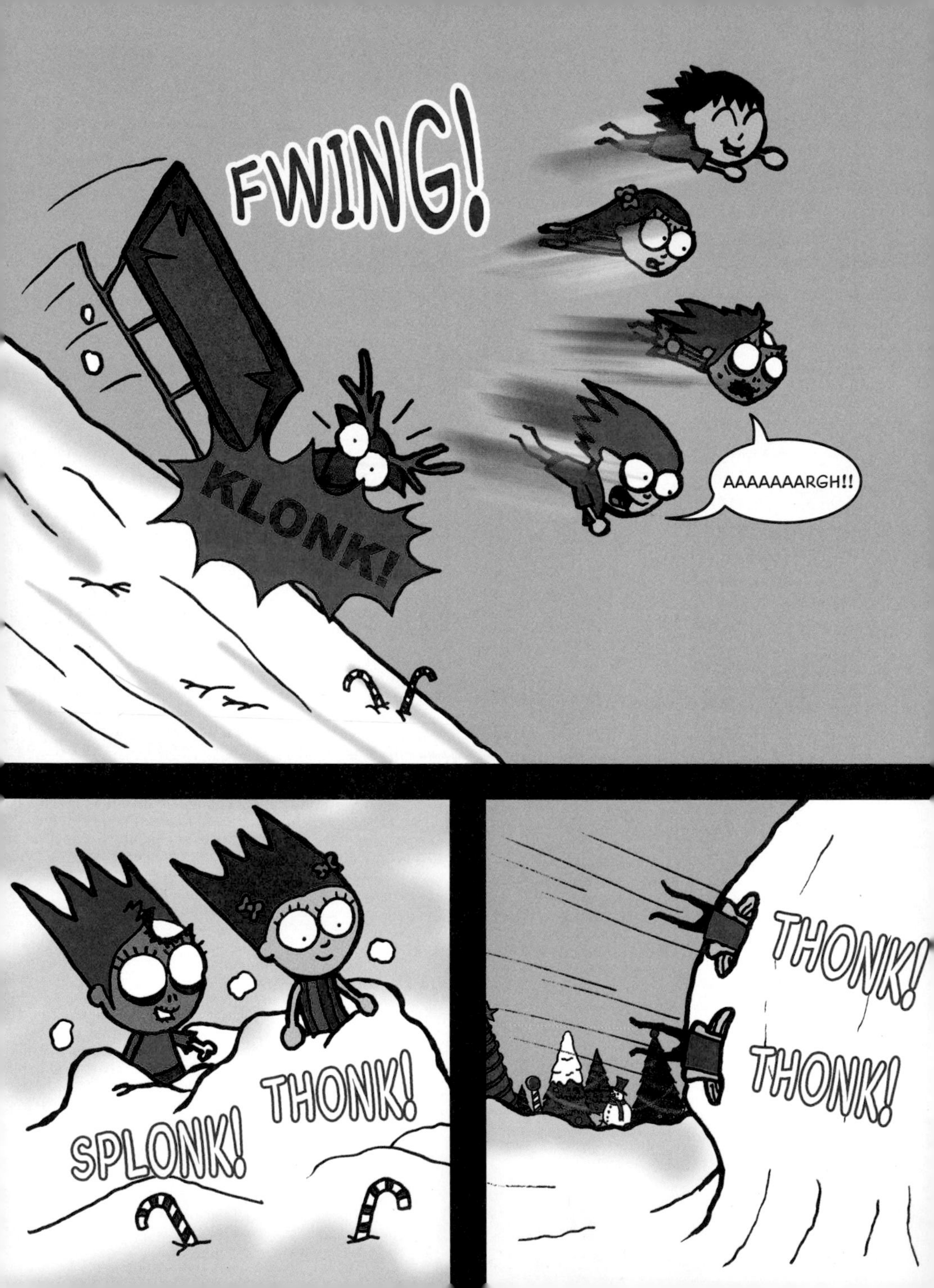
FWING!
KLONK!
AAAAAAARGH!!
THONK!
SPLONK!
THONK!
THONK!

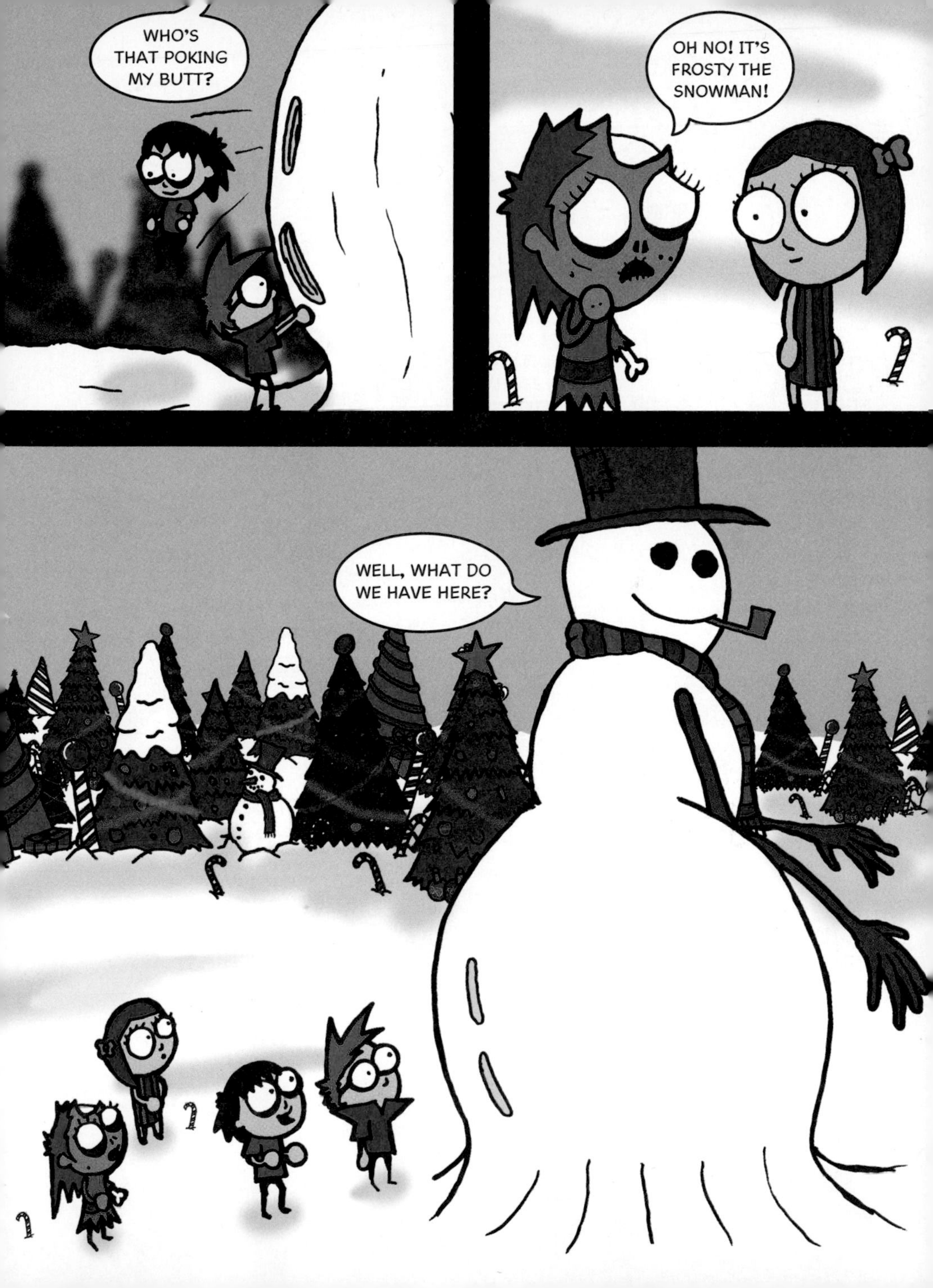
WHO'S THAT POKING MY BUTT?
OH NO! IT'S FROSTY THE SNOWMAN!
WELL, WHAT DO WE HAVE HERE?

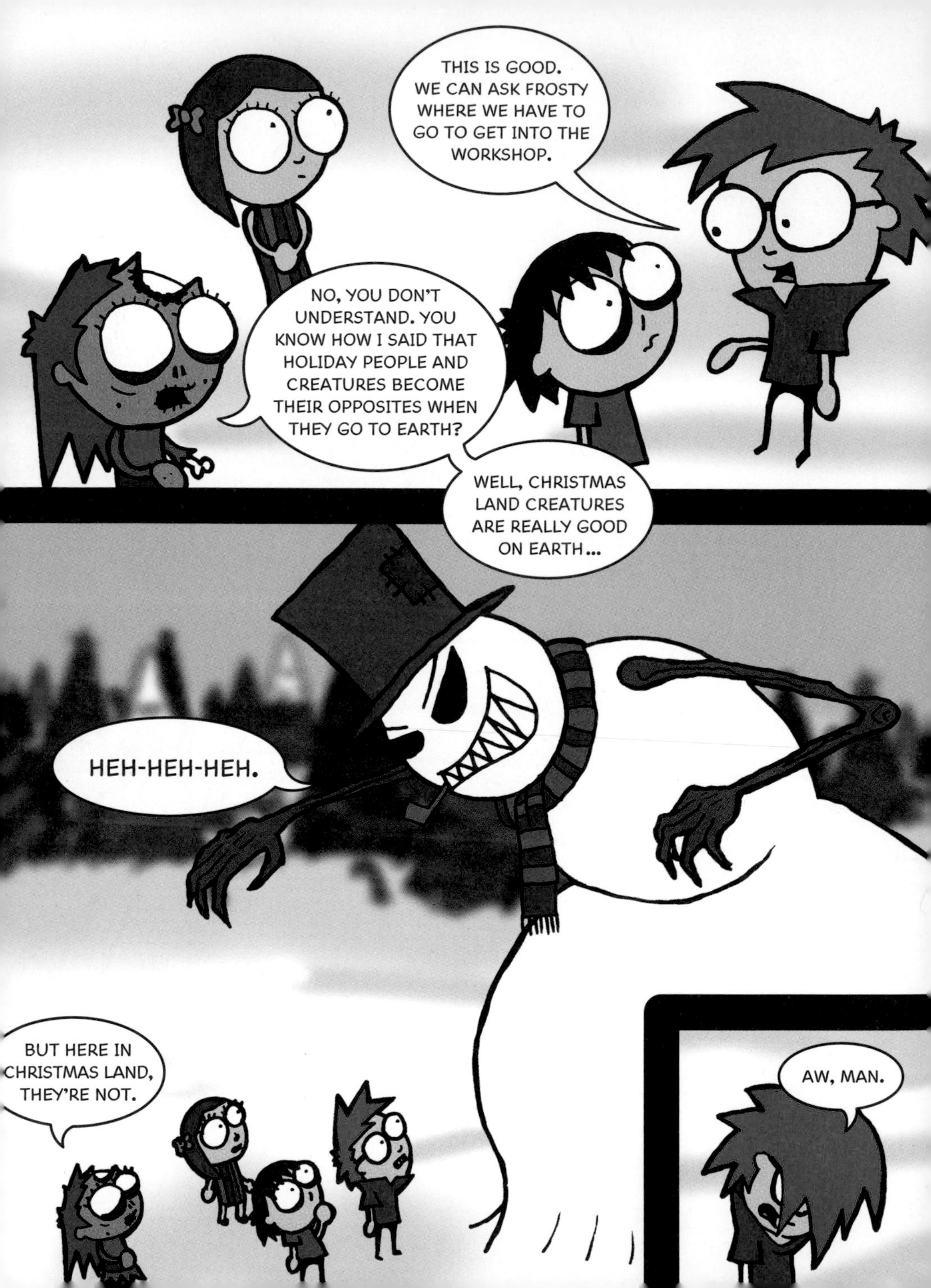
THIS IS GOOD. WE CAN ASK FROSTY WHERE WE HAVE TO GO TO GET INTO THE WORKSHOP.
NO, YOU DON'T UNDERSTAND. YOU KNOW HOW I SAID THAT HOLIDAY PEOPLE AND CREATURES BECOME THEIR OPPOSITES WHEN THEY GO TO EARTH?
WELL, CHRISTMAS LAND CREATURES ARE REALLY GOOD ON EARTH...
HEH-HEH-HEH.
BUT HERE IN CHRISTMAS LAND, THEY'RE NOT.
AW, MAN.

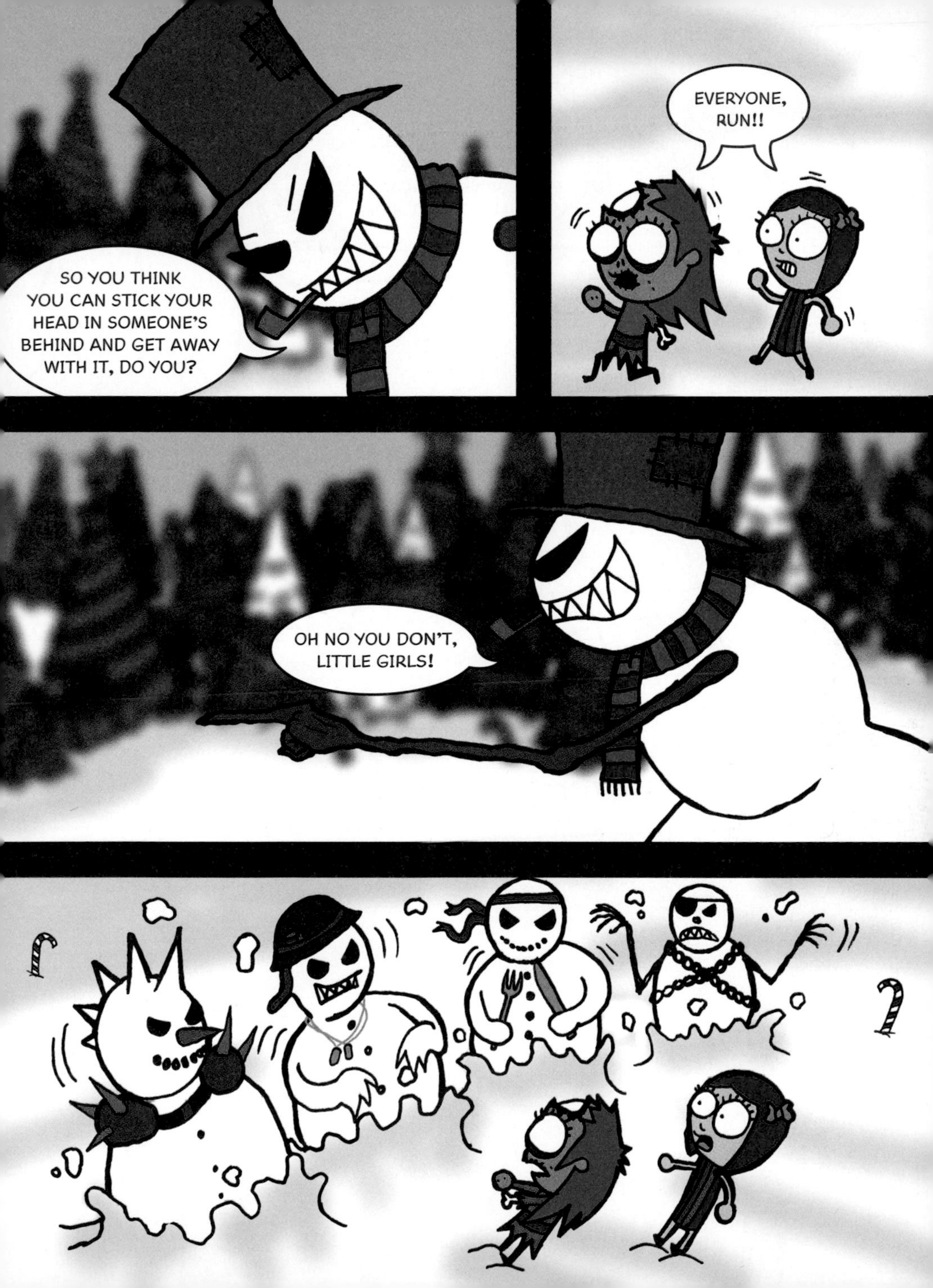
SO YOU THINK YOU CAN STICK YOUR HEAD IN SOMEONE'S BEHIND AND GET AWAY WITH IT, DO YOU?
EVERYONE, RUN!!
OH NO YOU DON'T, LITTLE GIRLS!

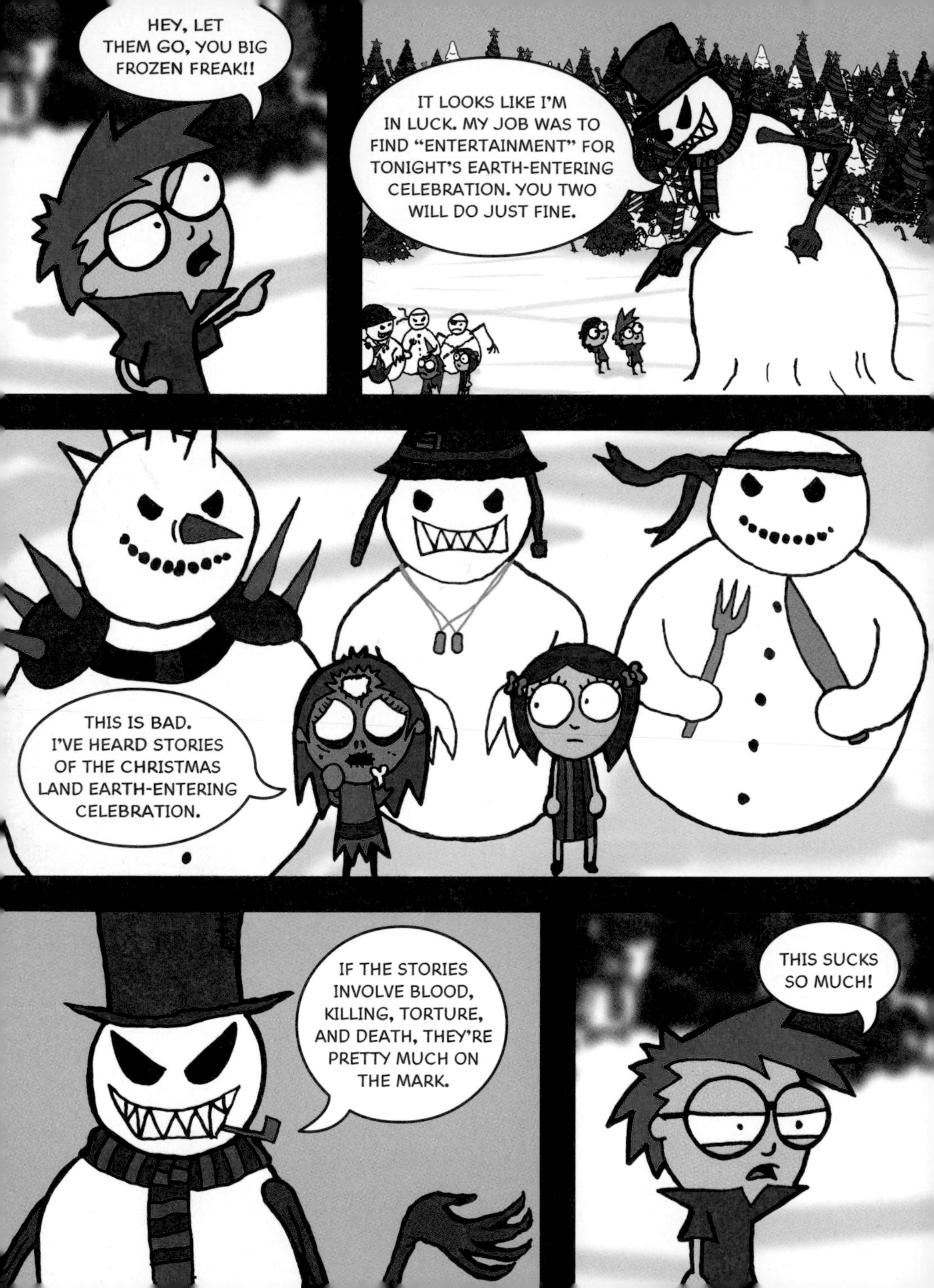

HEY, LET THEM GO, YOU BIG FROZEN FREAK!!
IT LOOKS LIKE I'M IN LUCK. MY JOB WAS TO FIND "ENTERTAINMENT" FOR TONIGHT'S EARTH-ENTERING CELEBRATION. YOU TWO WILL DO JUST FINE.
THIS IS BAD. I'VE HEARD STORIES OF THE CHRISTMAS LAND EARTH-ENTERING CELEBRATION.
IF THE STORIES INVOLVE BLOOD, KILLING, TORTURE, AND DEATH, THEY'RE PRETTY MUCH ON THE MARK.
THIS SUCKS SO MUCH!

CHAPTER THREE
THE EARTH-ENTERING CELEBRATION

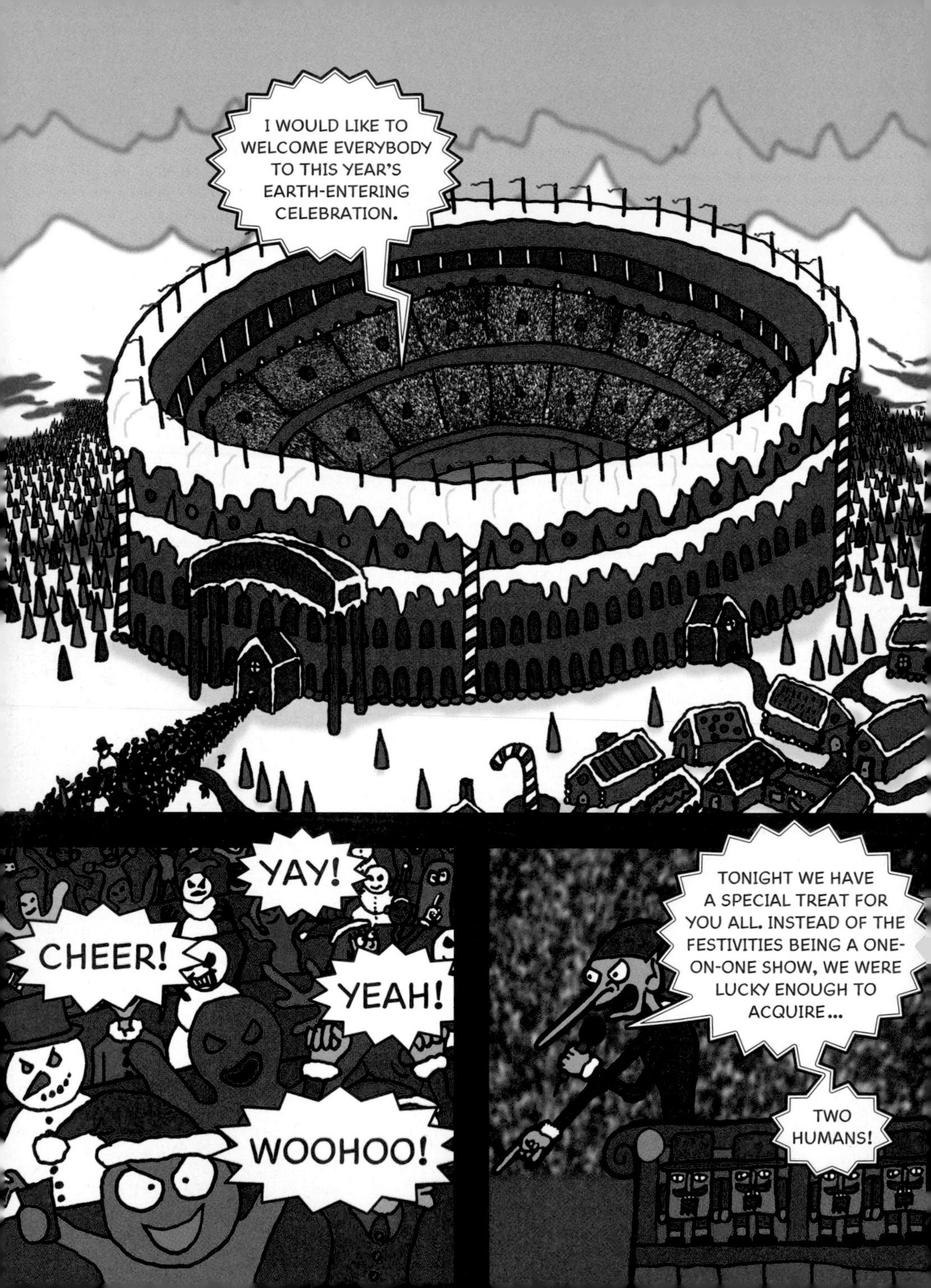
I WOULD LIKE TO WELCOME EVERYBODY TO THIS YEAR'S EARTH-ENTERING CELEBRATION.
YAY!
CHEER!
YEAH!
WOOHOO!
TONIGHT WE HAVE A SPECIAL TREAT FOR YOU ALL. INSTEAD OF THE FESTIVITIES BEING A ONE-ON-ONE SHOW, WE WERE LUCKY ENOUGH TO ACQUIRE...
TWO HUMANS!

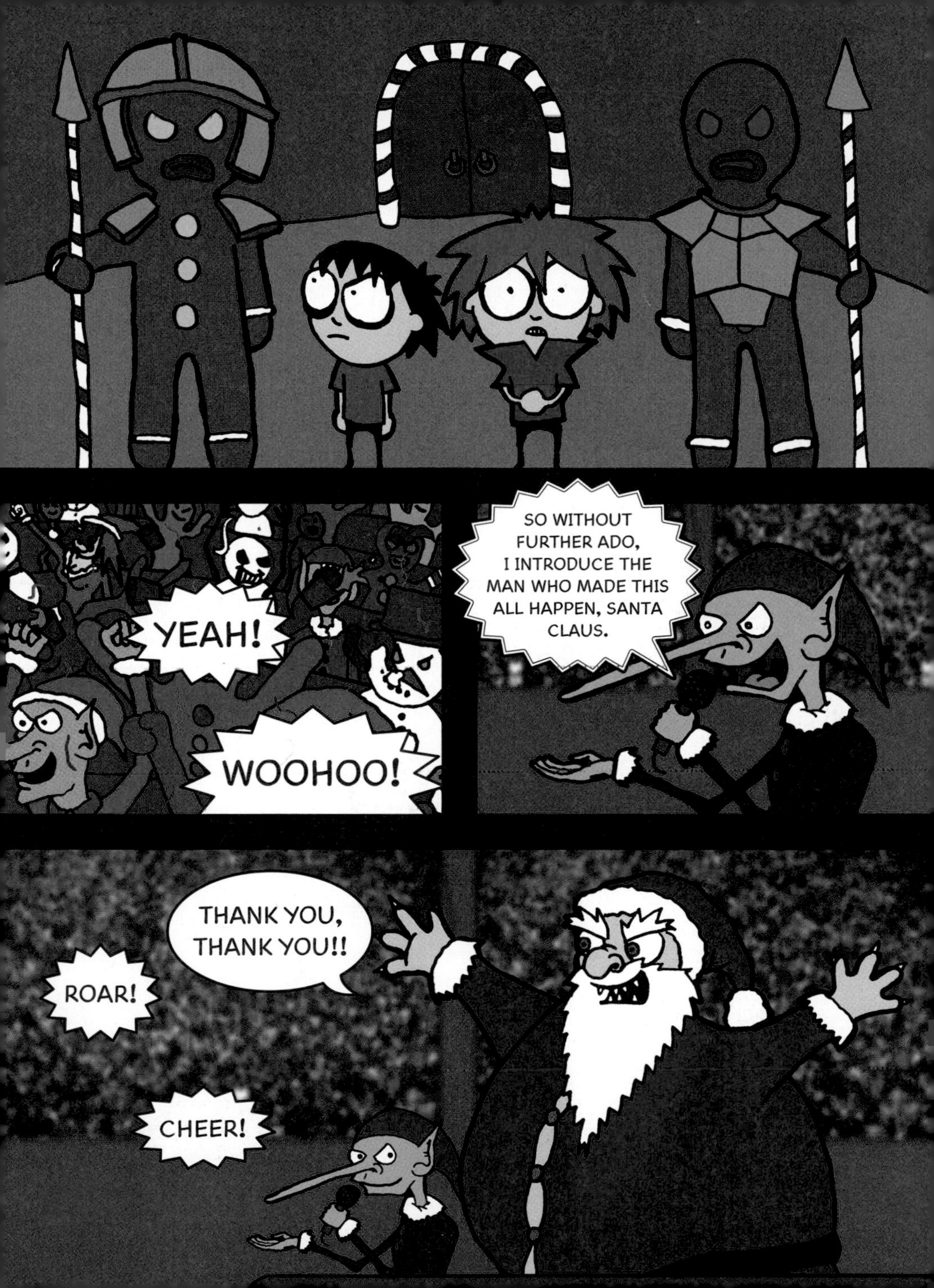
YEAH!
WOOHOO!
SO WITHOUT FURTHER ADO, I INTRODUCE THE MAN WHO MADE THIS ALL HAPPEN, SANTA CLAUS.
THANK YOU, THANK YOU!!
ROAR!
CHEER!

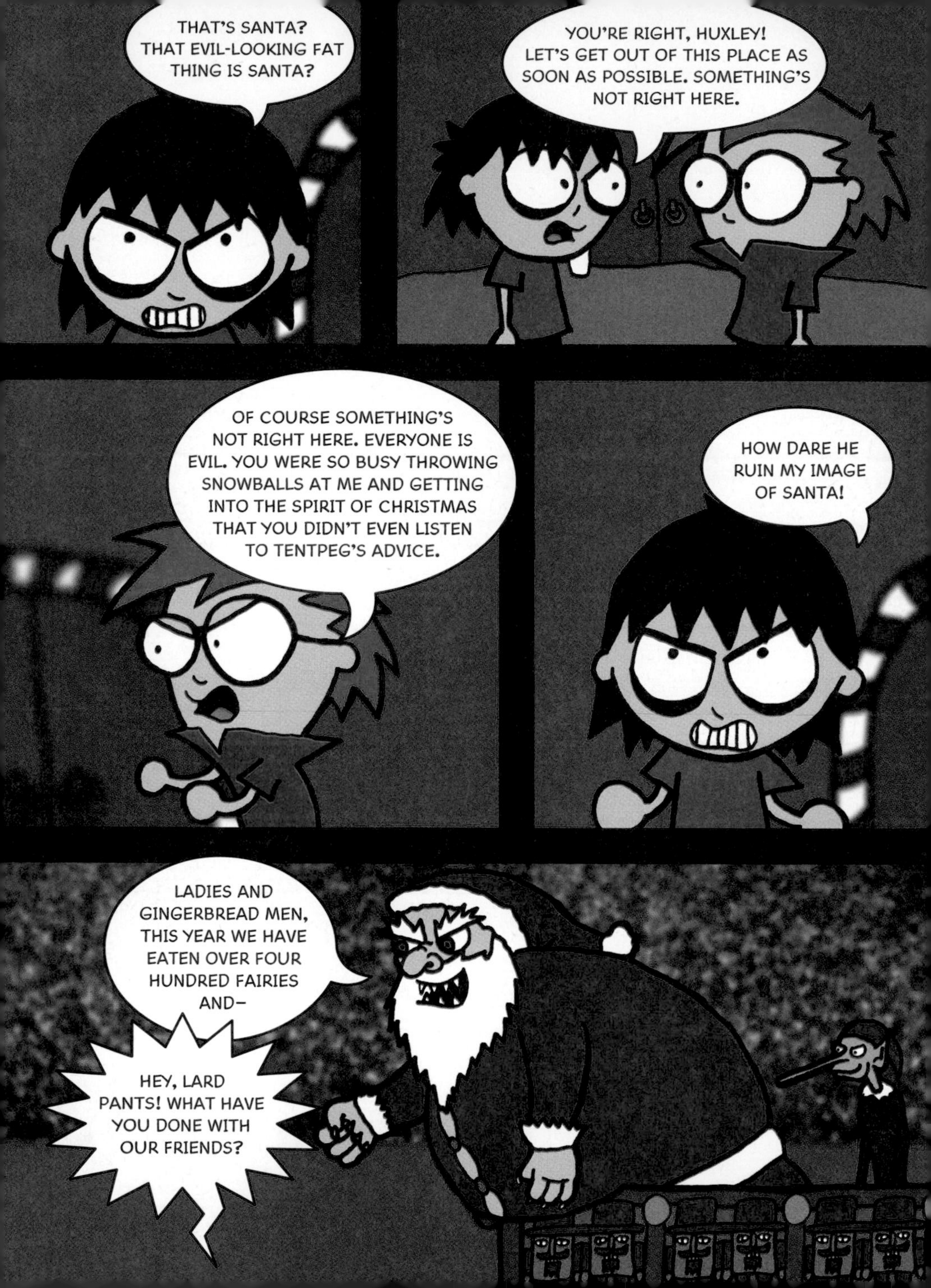
THAT'S SANTA? THAT EVIL-LOOKING FAT THING IS SANTA?
YOU'RE RIGHT, HUXLEY! LET'S GET OUT OF THIS PLACE AS SOON AS POSSIBLE. SOMETHING'S NOT RIGHT HERE.
OF COURSE SOMETHING'S NOT RIGHT HERE. EVERYONE IS EVIL. YOU WERE SO BUSY THROWING SNOWBALLS AT ME AND GETTING INTO THE SPIRIT OF CHRISTMAS THAT YOU DIDN'T EVEN LISTEN TO TENTPEG'S ADVICE.
HOW DARE HE RUIN MY IMAGE OF SANTA!
LADIES AND GINGERBREAD MEN, THIS YEAR WE HAVE EATEN OVER FOUR HUNDRED FAIRIES AND–
HEY, LARD PANTS! WHAT HAVE YOU DONE WITH OUR FRIENDS?

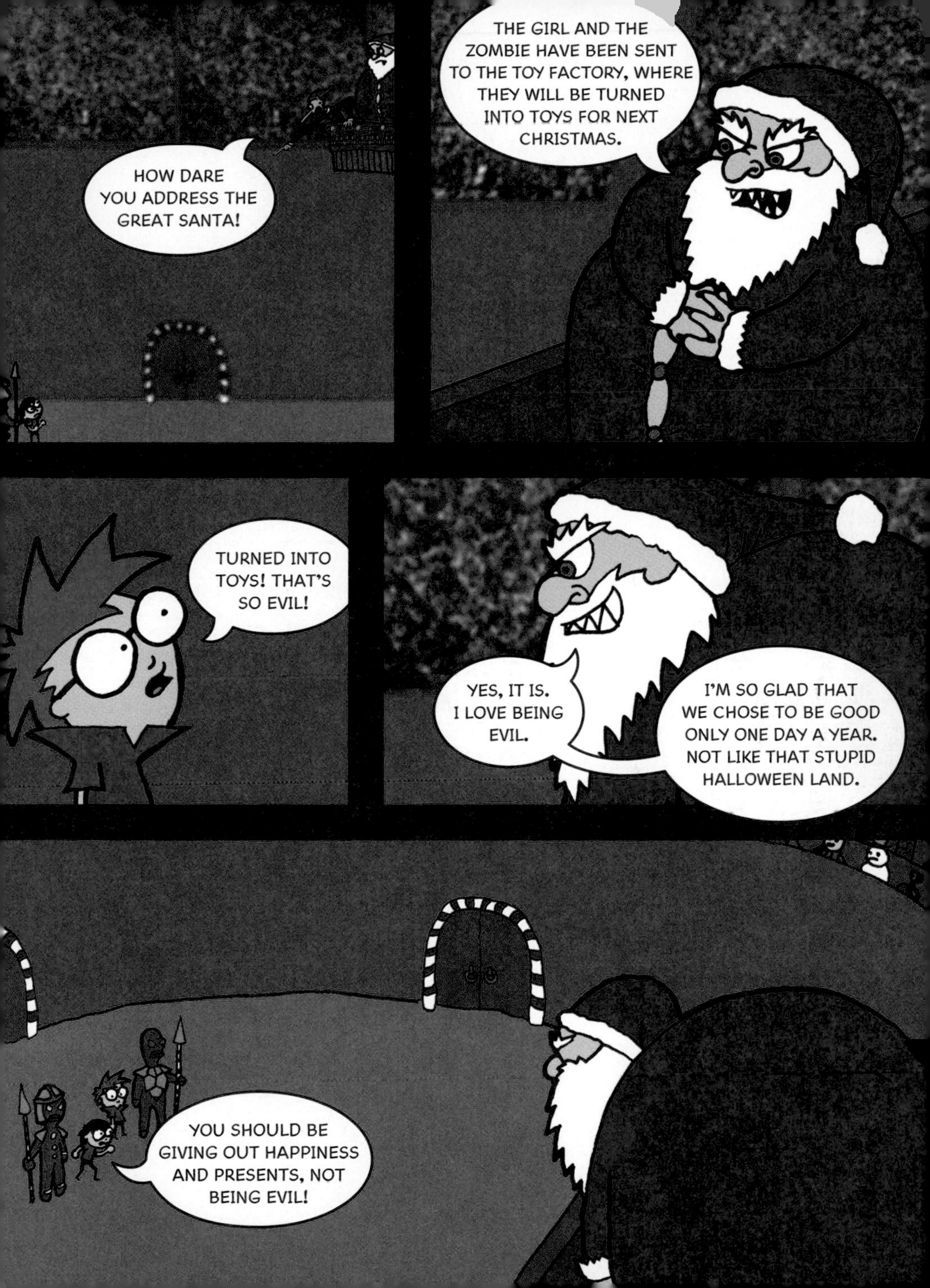
HOW DARE YOU ADDRESS THE GREAT SANTA!
THE GIRL AND THE ZOMBIE HAVE BEEN SENT TO THE TOY FACTORY, WHERE THEY WILL BE TURNED INTO TOYS FOR NEXT CHRISTMAS.
TURNED INTO TOYS! THAT'S SO EVIL!
YES, IT IS. I LOVE BEING EVIL.
I'M SO GLAD THAT WE CHOSE TO BE GOOD ONLY ONE DAY A YEAR. NOT LIKE THAT STUPID HALLOWEEN LAND.
YOU SHOULD BE GIVING OUT HAPPINESS AND PRESENTS, NOT BEING EVIL!

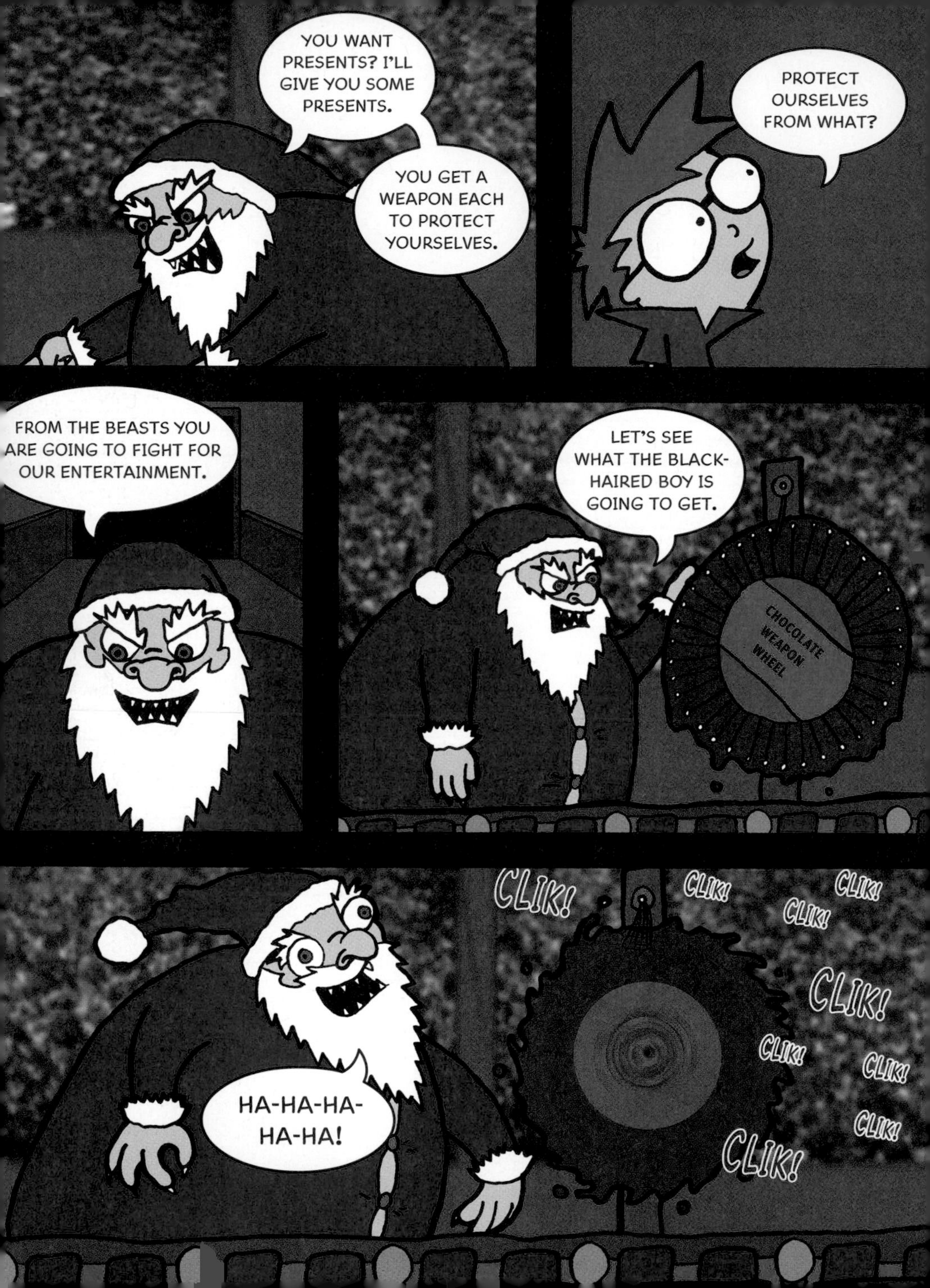
YOU WANT PRESENTS? I'LL GIVE YOU SOME PRESENTS.
YOU GET A WEAPON EACH TO PROTECT YOURSELVES.
PROTECT OURSELVES FROM WHAT?
FROM THE BEASTS YOU ARE GOING TO FIGHT FOR OUR ENTERTAINMENT.
LET'S SEE WHAT THE BLACK-HAIRED BOY IS GOING TO GET.
CHOCOLATE WEAPON WHEEL
HA-HA-HA-HA-HA!
CLIK! CLIK! CLIK! CLIK! CLIK! CLIK! CLIK! CLIK! CLIK!

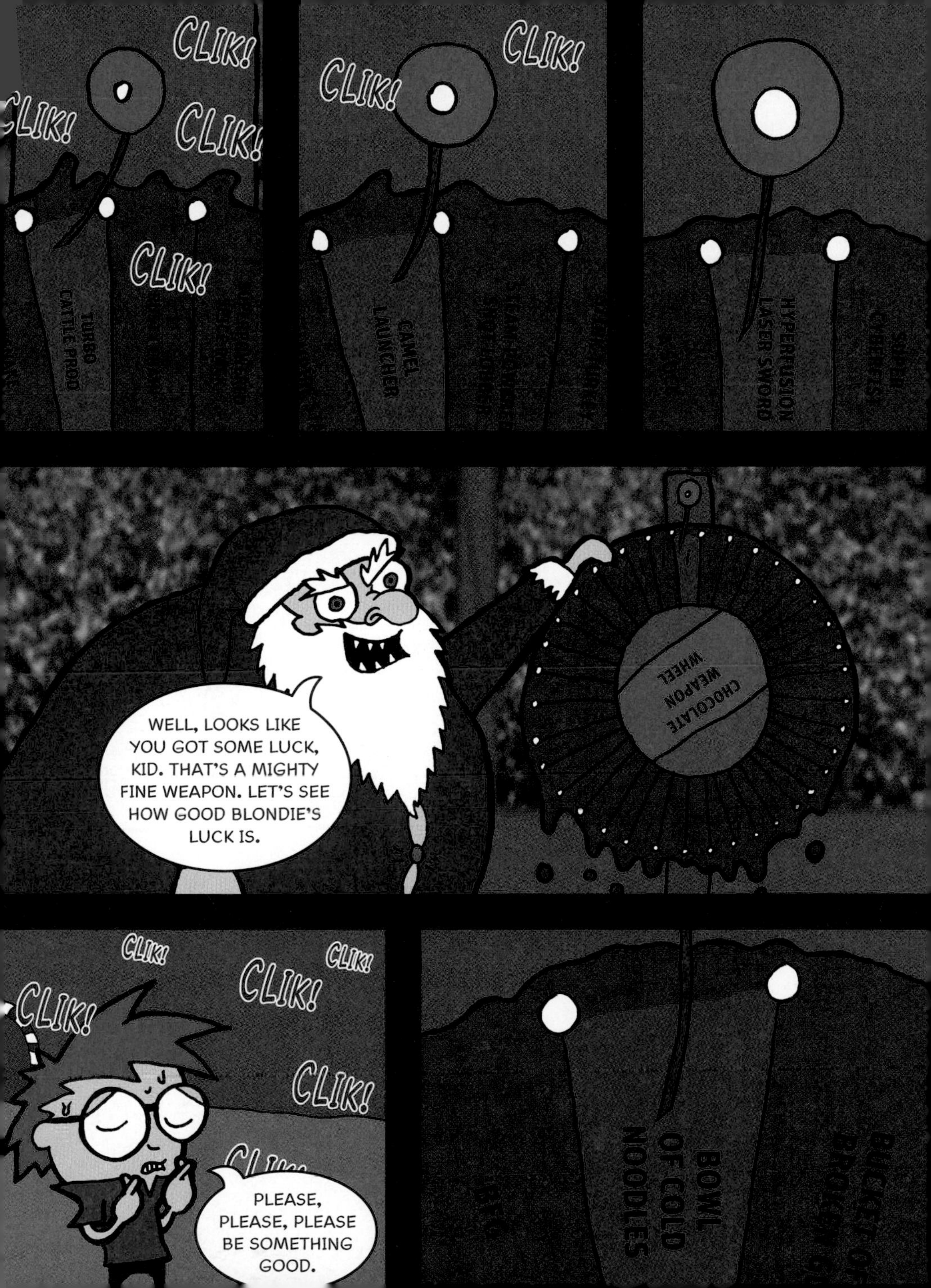
CLIK!
CLIK!
CLIK!
CLIK!
TURBO CATTLE PROD
CLIK!
CLIK!
CAMEL LAUNCHER
HYPERFUSION LASER SWORD
CHOCOLATE WEAPON WHEEL
WELL, LOOKS LIKE YOU GOT SOME LUCK, KID. THAT'S A MIGHTY FINE WEAPON. LET'S SEE HOW GOOD BLONDIE'S LUCK IS.
CLIK!
CLIK!
CLIK!
CLIK!
CLIK!
PLEASE, PLEASE, PLEASE BE SOMETHING GOOD.
BOWL OF COLD NOODLES

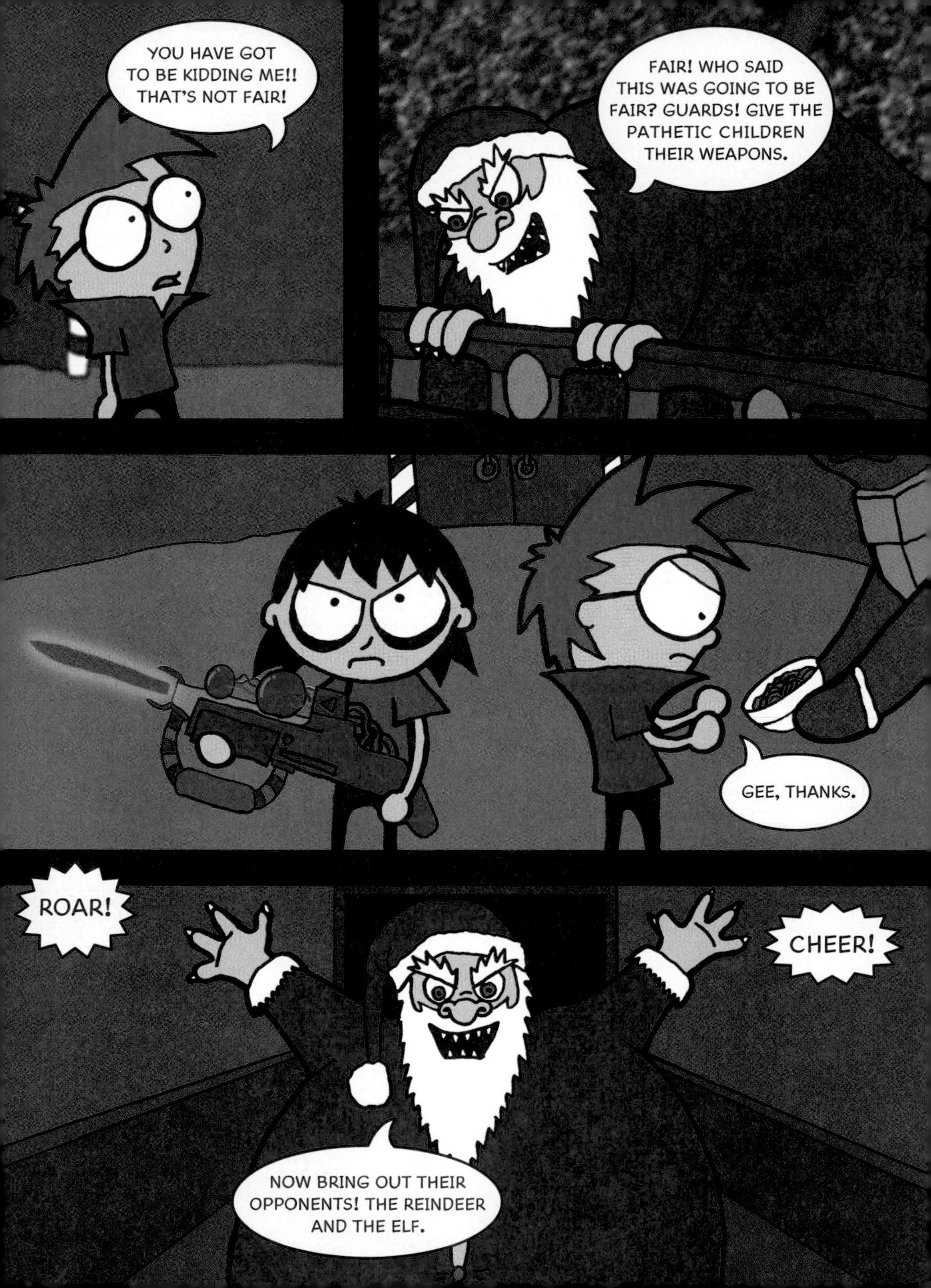
YOU HAVE GOT TO BE KIDDING ME!! THAT'S NOT FAIR!
FAIR! WHO SAID THIS WAS GOING TO BE FAIR? GUARDS! GIVE THE PATHETIC CHILDREN THEIR WEAPONS.
GEE, THANKS.
ROAR!
CHEER!
NOW BRING OUT THEIR OPPONENTS! THE REINDEER AND THE ELF.

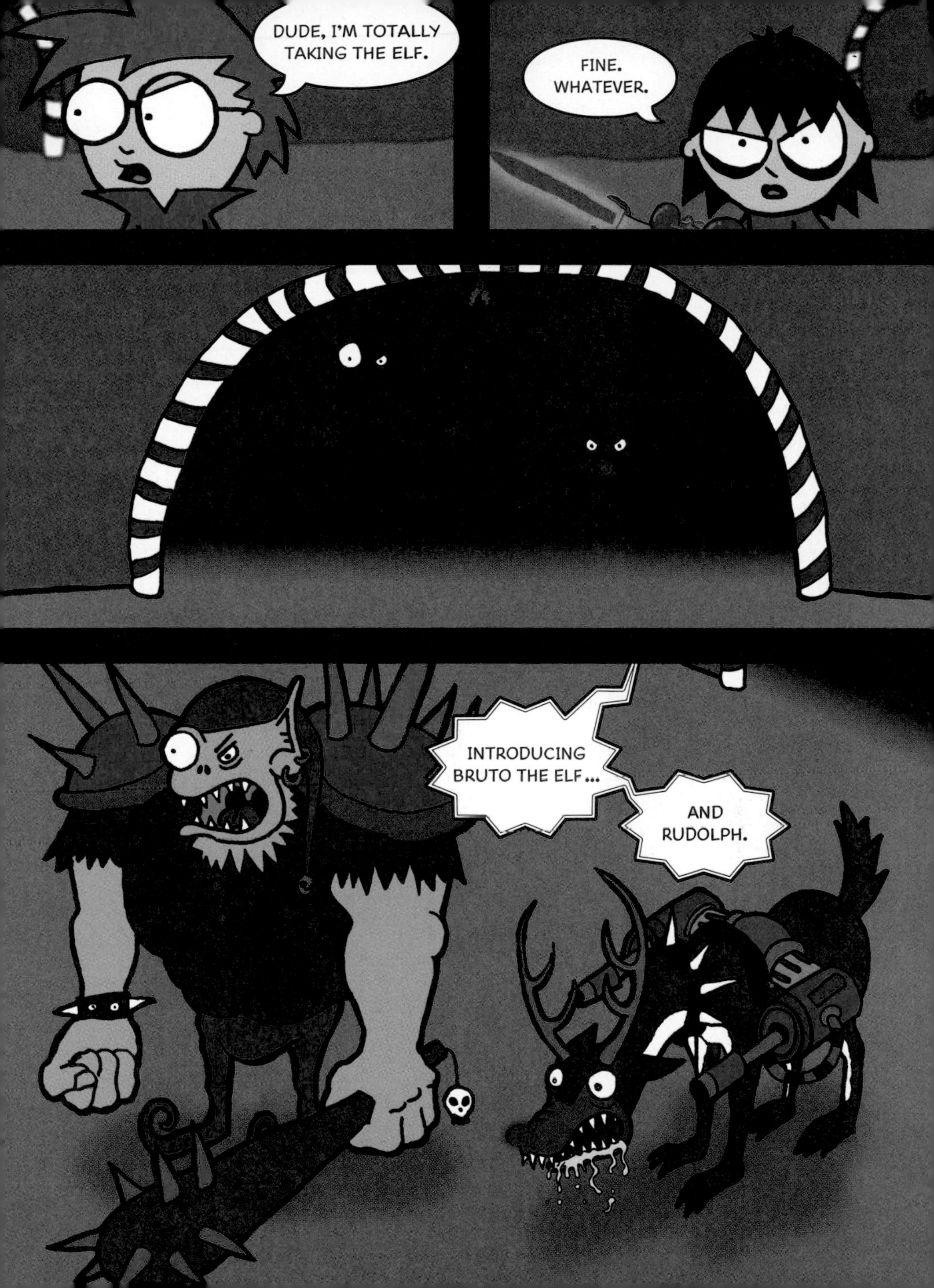
DUDE, I'M TOTALLY TAKING THE ELF.
FINE. WHATEVER.
INTRODUCING BRUTO THE ELF...
AND RUDOLPH.

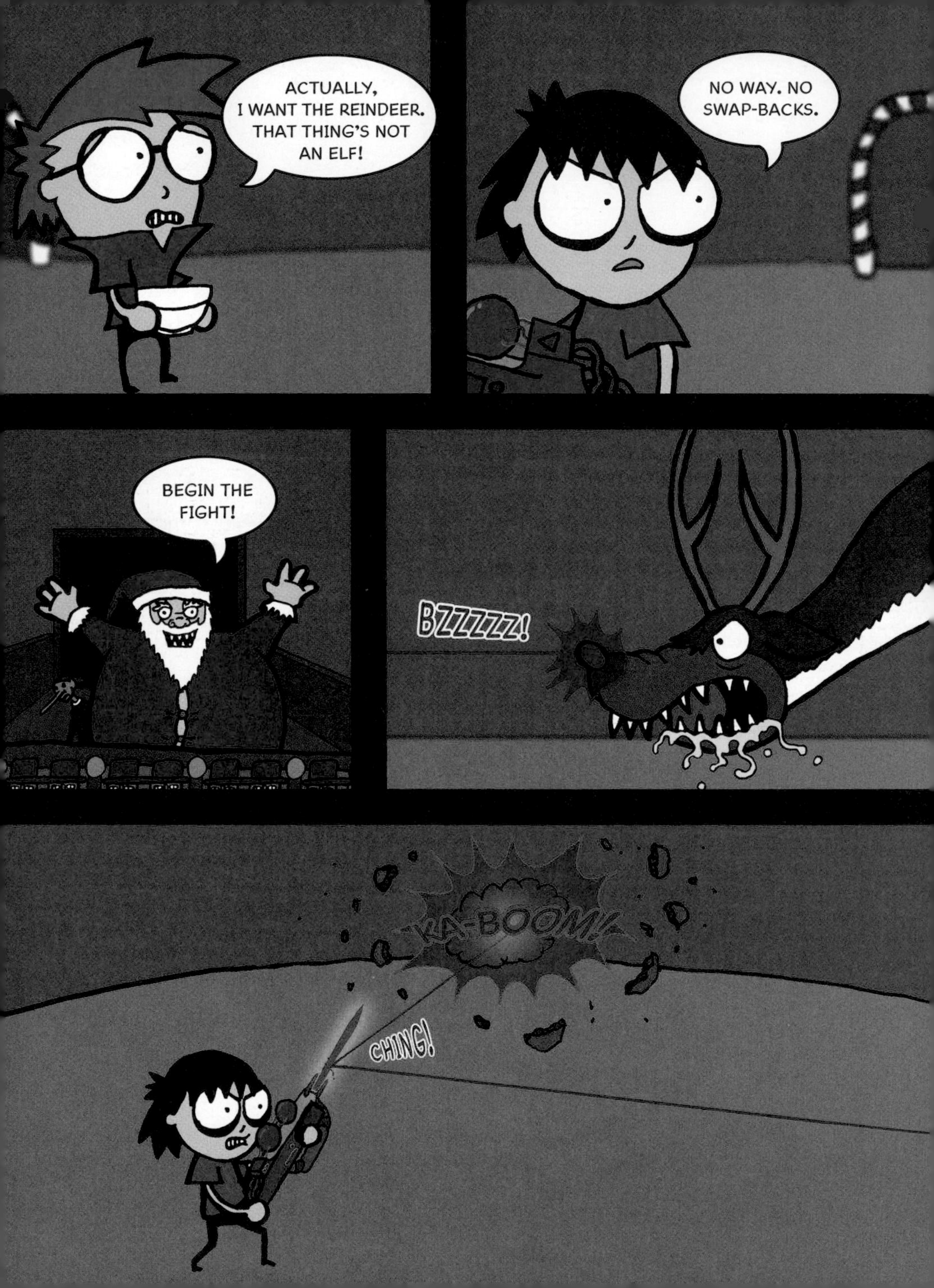
ACTUALLY, I WANT THE REINDEER. THAT THING'S NOT AN ELF!
NO WAY. NO SWAP-BACKS.
BEGIN THE FIGHT!
BZZZZZZ!
KA-BOOM!
CHING!

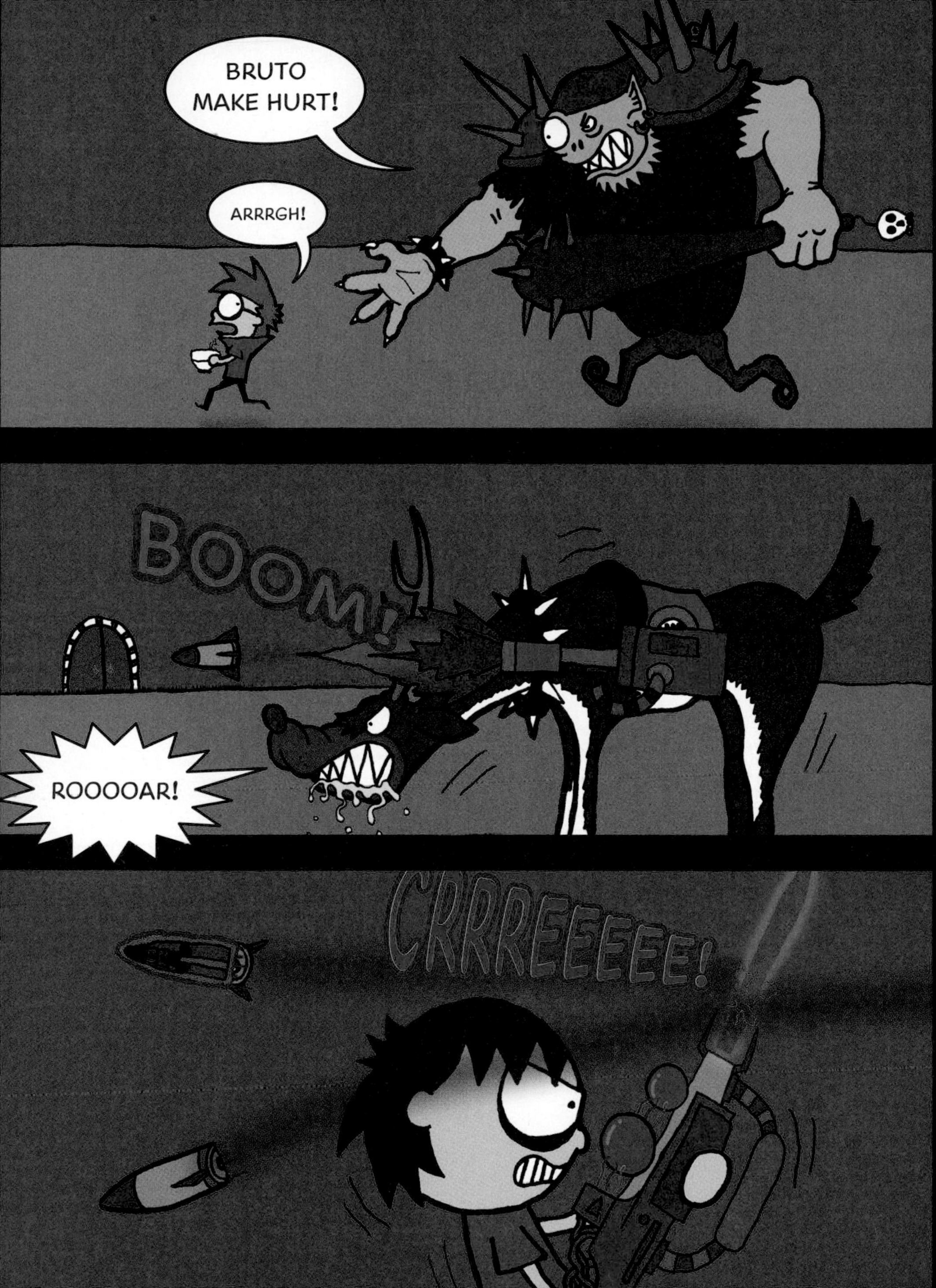
BRUTO MAKE HURT!
ARRRGH!
BOOM!
ROOOOAR!
CRRREEEEEE!

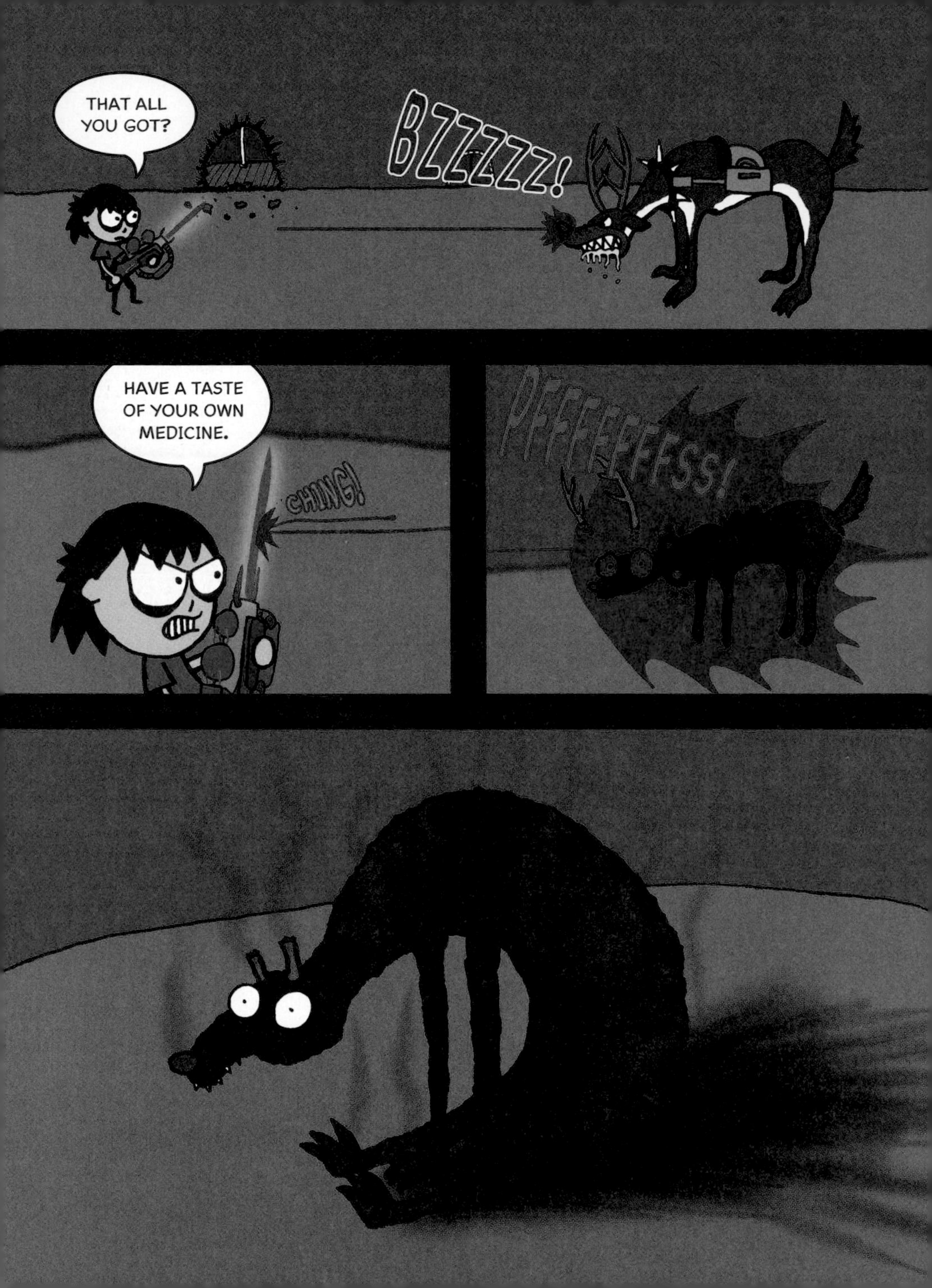
THAT ALL YOU GOT?
BZZZZZZ!
HAVE A TASTE OF YOUR OWN MEDICINE.
CHING!
PFFFFFFFFSSS!

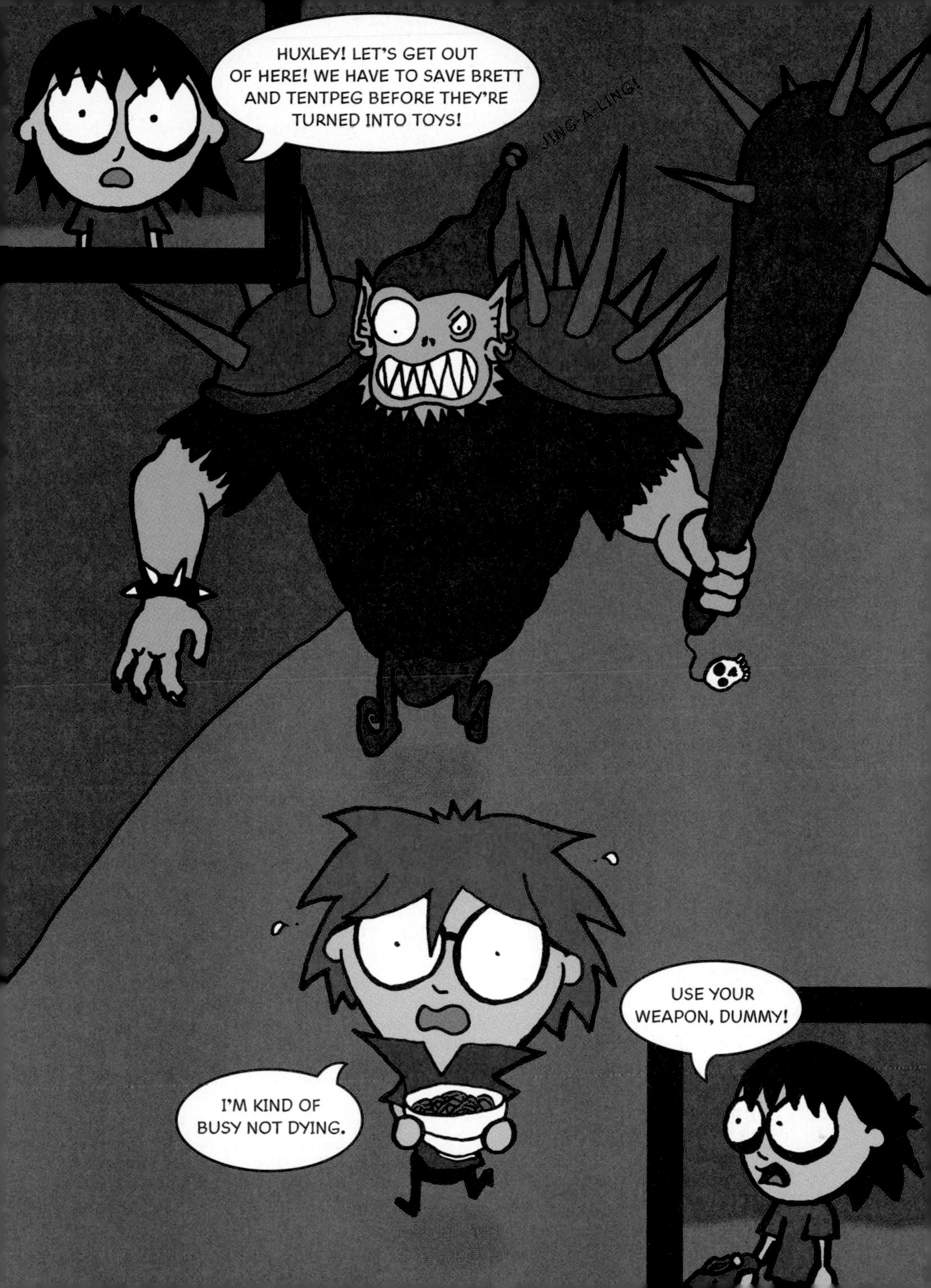
HUXLEY! LET'S GET OUT OF HERE! WE HAVE TO SAVE BRETT AND TENTPEG BEFORE THEY'RE TURNED INTO TOYS!
JING-A-LING!
USE YOUR WEAPON, DUMMY!
I'M KIND OF BUSY NOT DYING.

SPLOOT!

THIS IS SO STUPID! WHAT COULD A BOWL OF COLD NOODLES POSSIBLY DO?

FWING!

ARRGH! BRUTO ALLERGIC TO NOODLES!

WOW! WHAT ARE THE ODDS?

SPLORTCH

QUICK! THIS WAY!

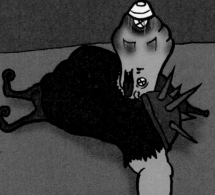

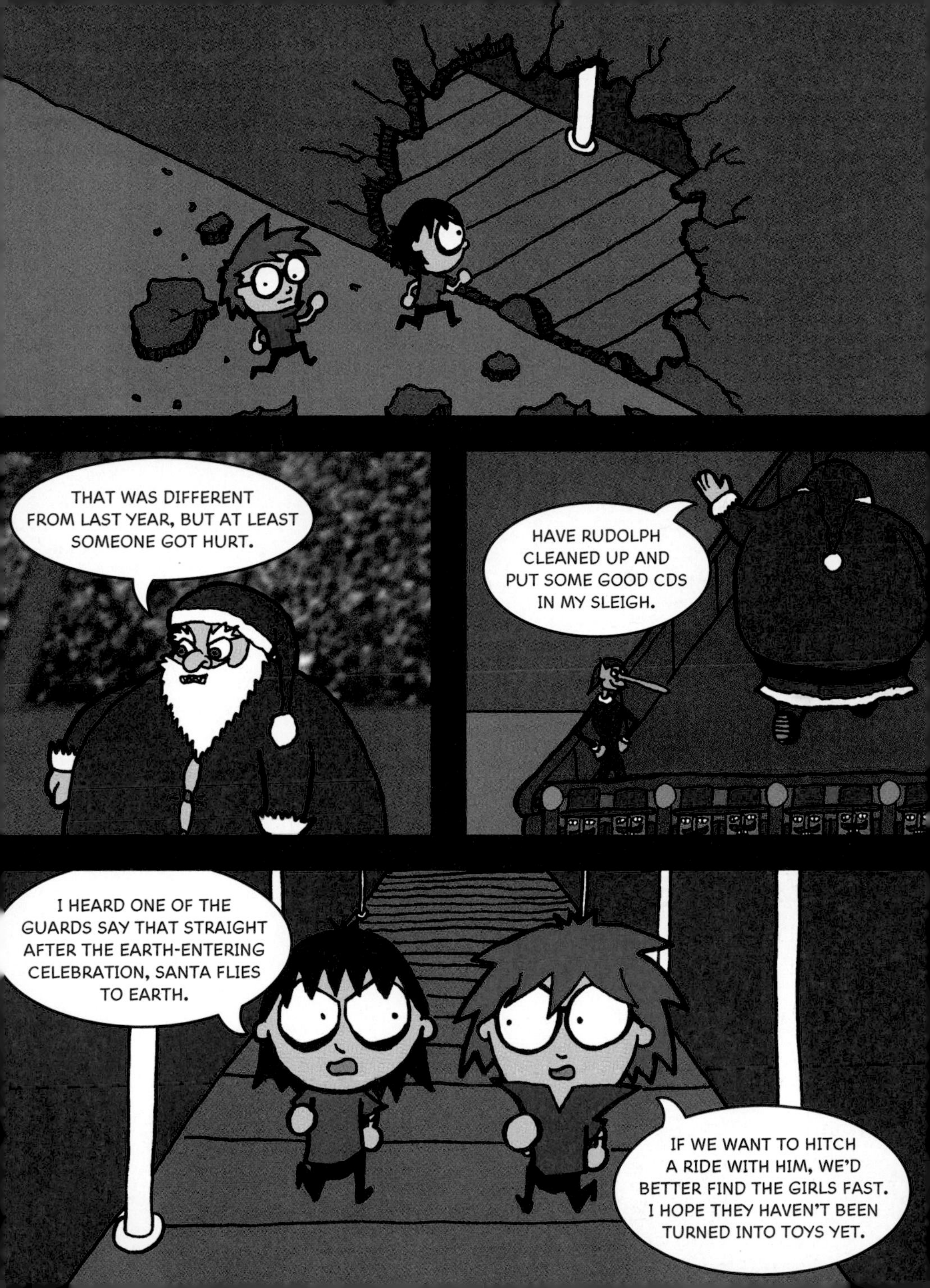
THAT WAS DIFFERENT FROM LAST YEAR, BUT AT LEAST SOMEONE GOT HURT.
HAVE RUDOLPH CLEANED UP AND PUT SOME GOOD CDS IN MY SLEIGH.
I HEARD ONE OF THE GUARDS SAY THAT STRAIGHT AFTER THE EARTH-ENTERING CELEBRATION, SANTA FLIES TO EARTH.
IF WE WANT TO HITCH A RIDE WITH HIM, WE'D BETTER FIND THE GIRLS FAST. I HOPE THEY HAVEN'T BEEN TURNED INTO TOYS YET.

CHAPTER FOUR

GOOD-BYE CHRISTMAS, HELLO TROUBLE

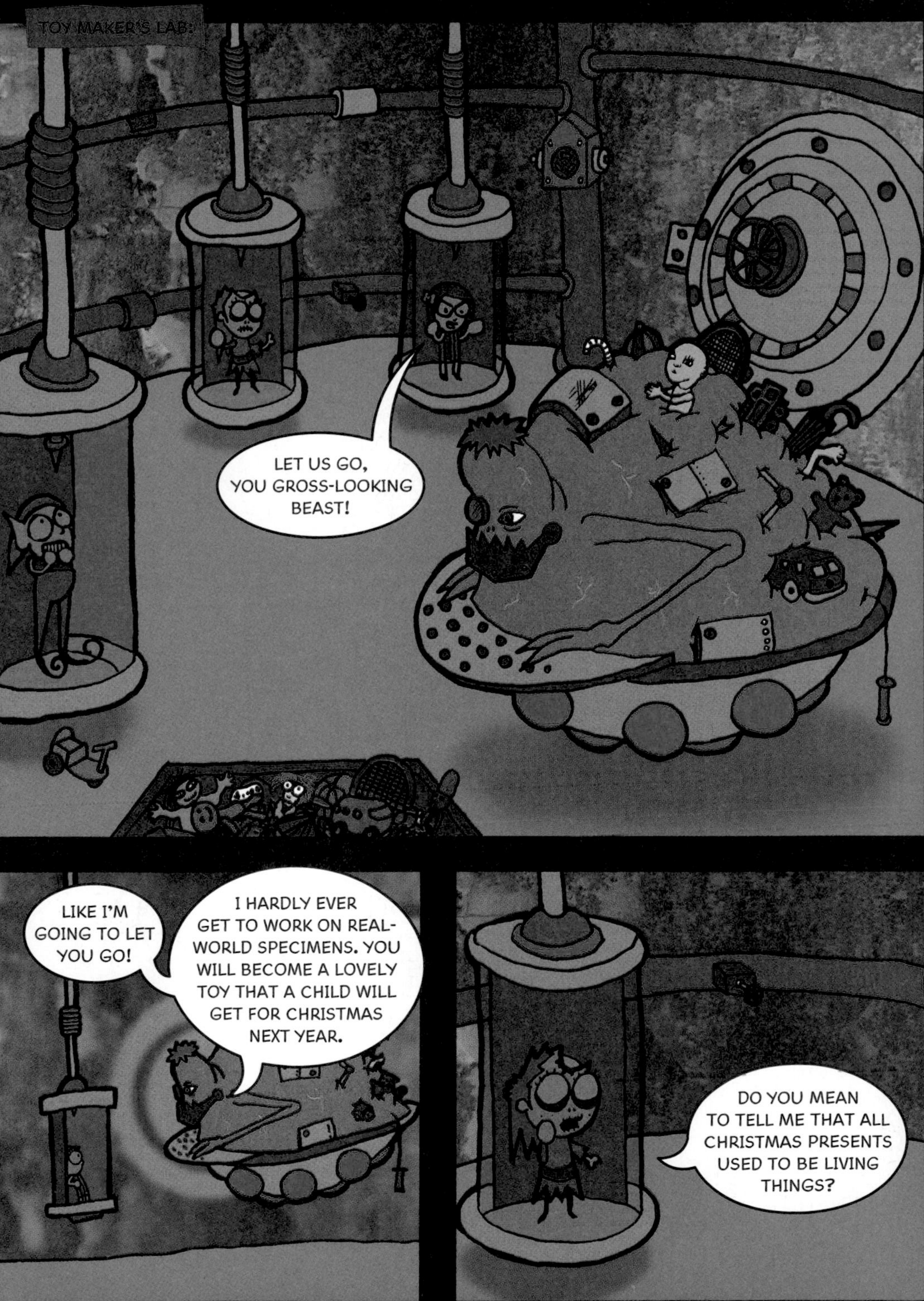
TOY MAKER'S LAB:
LET US GO, YOU GROSS-LOOKING BEAST!
LIKE I'M GOING TO LET YOU GO!
I HARDLY EVER GET TO WORK ON REAL-WORLD SPECIMENS. YOU WILL BECOME A LOVELY TOY THAT A CHILD WILL GET FOR CHRISTMAS NEXT YEAR.
DO YOU MEAN TO TELL ME THAT ALL CHRISTMAS PRESENTS USED TO BE LIVING THINGS?

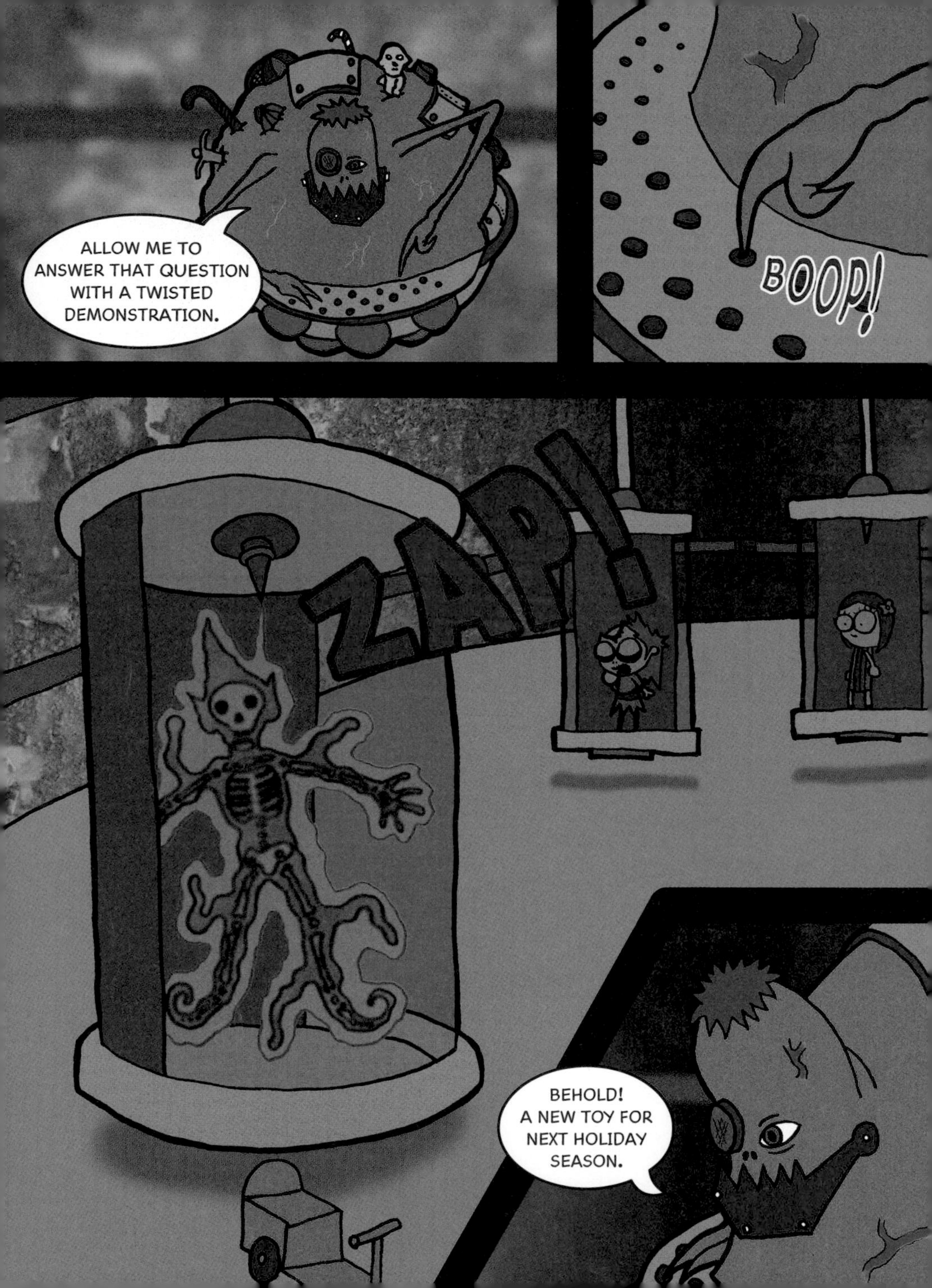
ALLOW ME TO ANSWER THAT QUESTION WITH A TWISTED DEMONSTRATION.
BOOP!
ZAP!
BEHOLD! A NEW TOY FOR NEXT HOLIDAY SEASON.

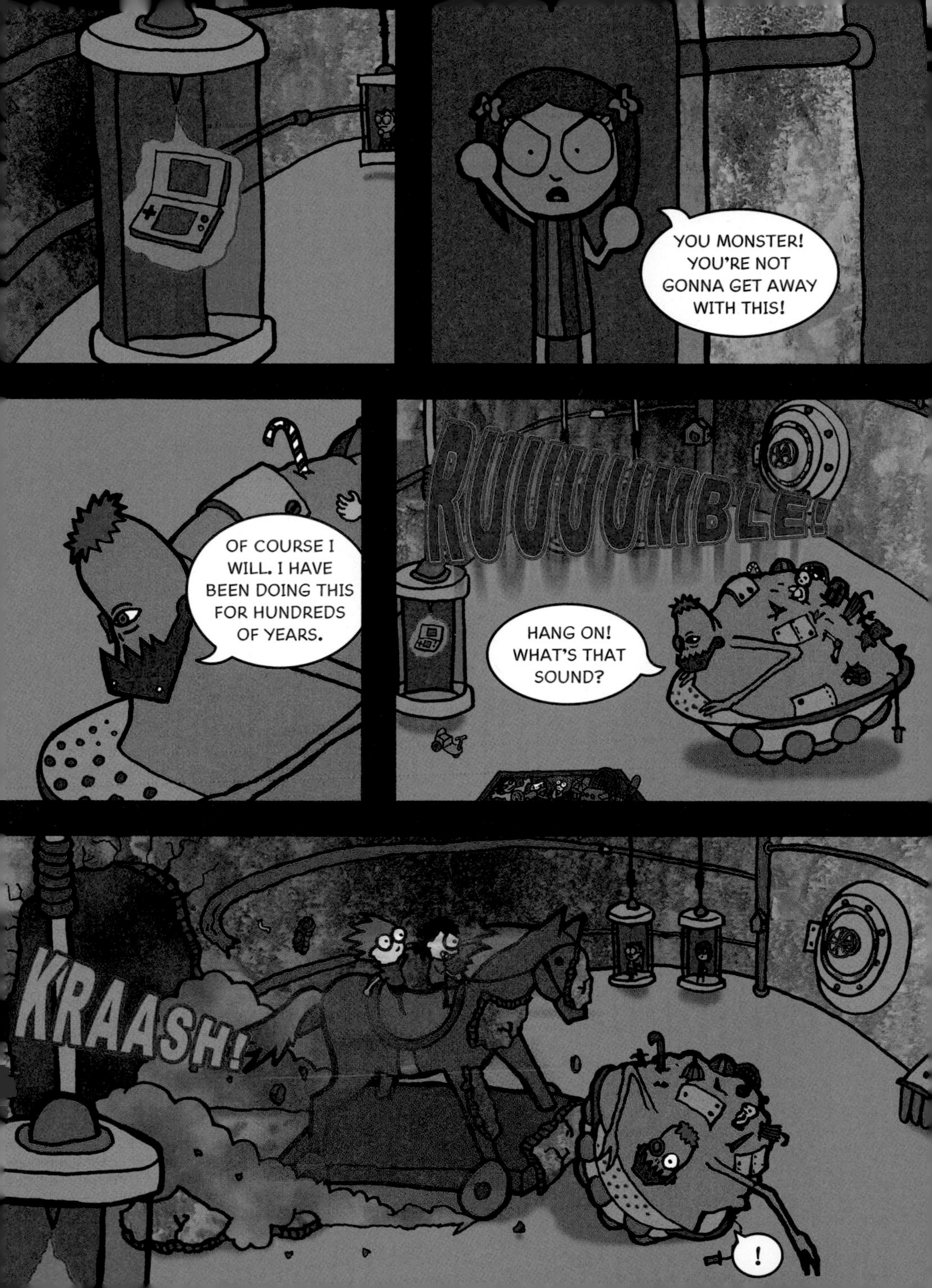
YOU MONSTER! YOU'RE NOT GONNA GET AWAY WITH THIS!
OF COURSE I WILL. I HAVE BEEN DOING THIS FOR HUNDREDS OF YEARS.
RUUUUUMBLE!
HANG ON! WHAT'S THAT SOUND?
KRAASH!
!

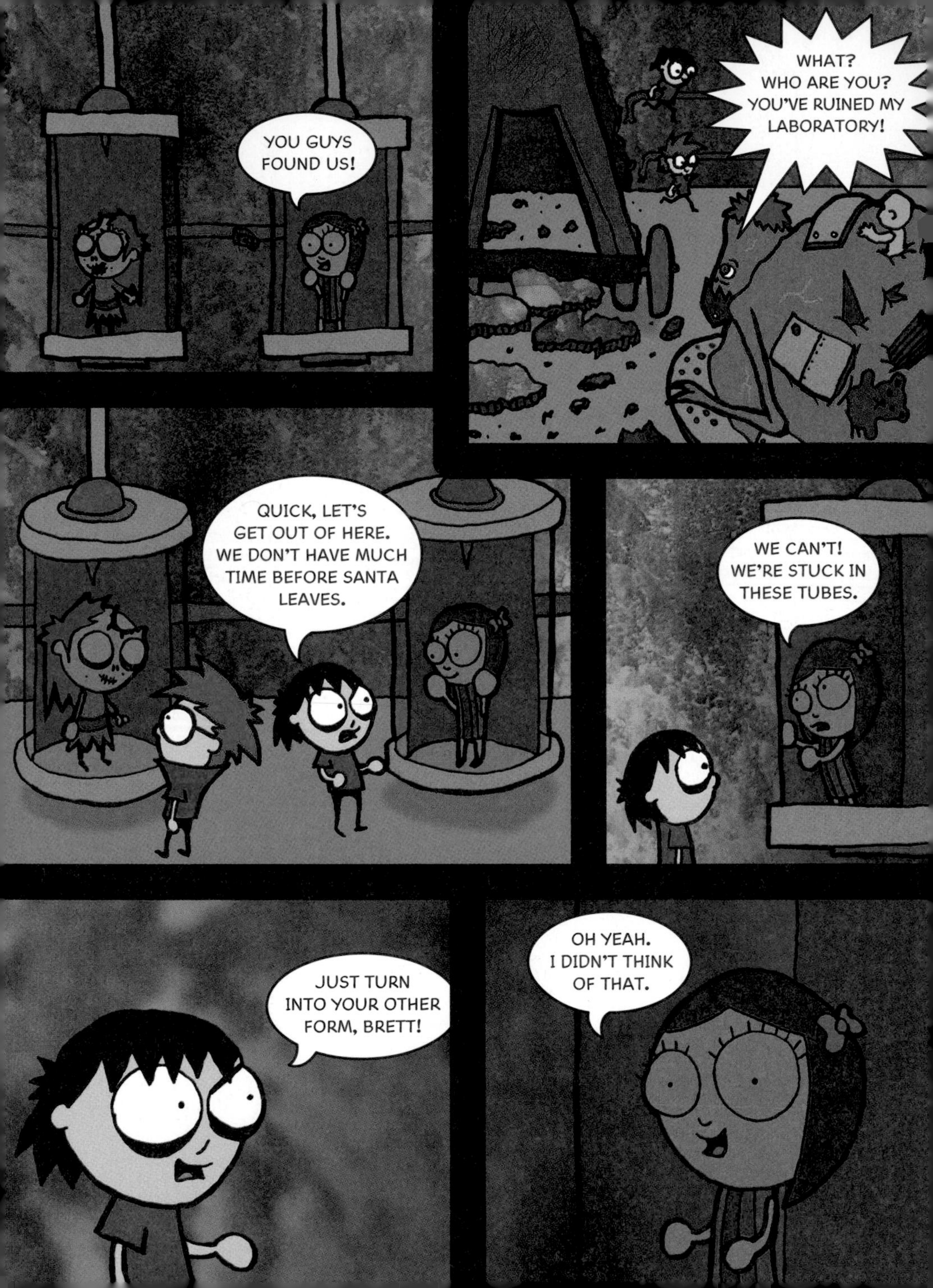
YOU GUYS FOUND US!
WHAT? WHO ARE YOU? YOU'VE RUINED MY LABORATORY!
QUICK, LET'S GET OUT OF HERE. WE DON'T HAVE MUCH TIME BEFORE SANTA LEAVES.
WE CAN'T! WE'RE STUCK IN THESE TUBES.
JUST TURN INTO YOUR OTHER FORM, BRETT!
OH YEAH. I DIDN'T THINK OF THAT.

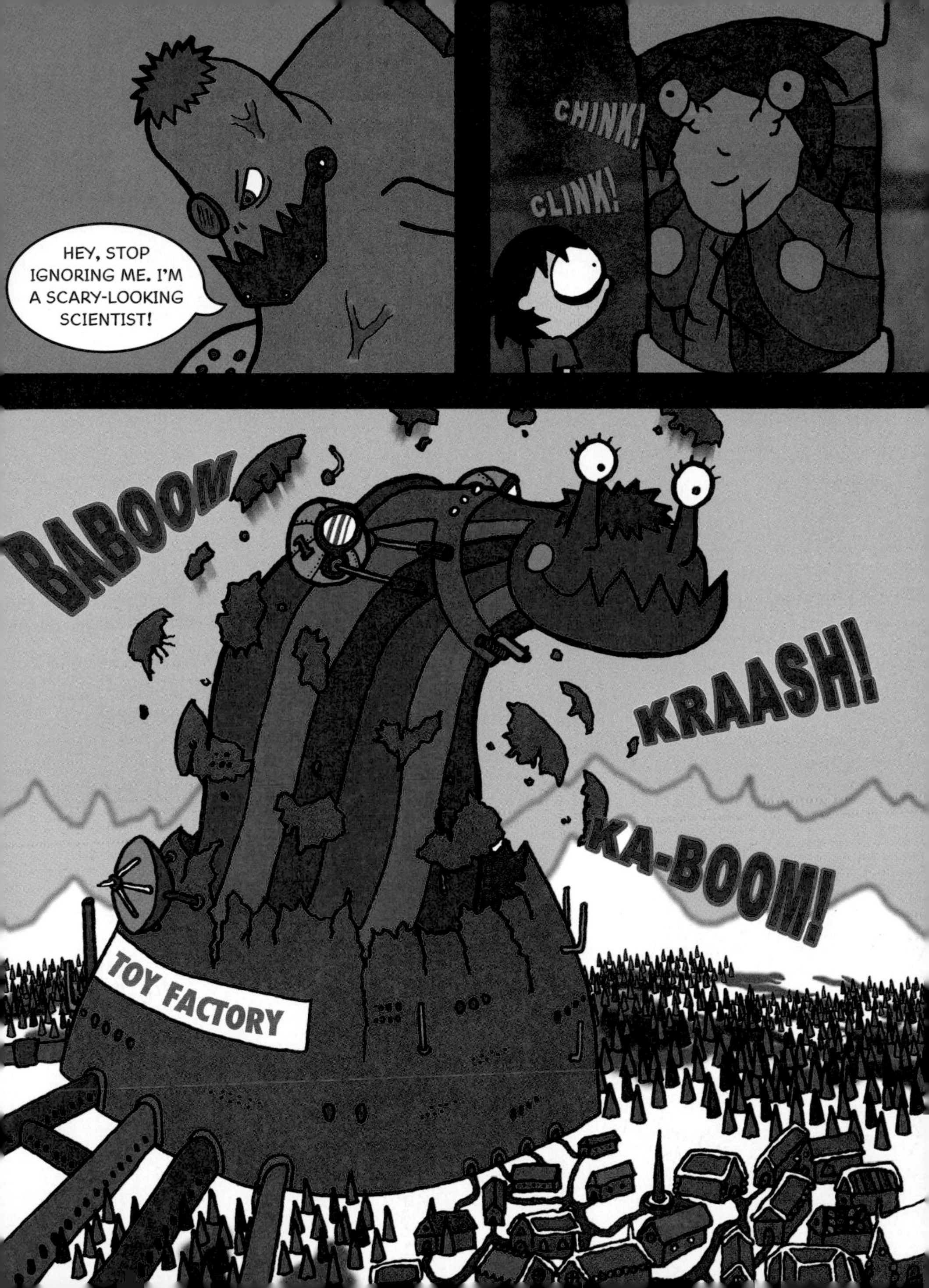
HEY, STOP IGNORING ME. I'M A SCARY-LOOKING SCIENTIST!
CHINK!
CLINK!
BABOOM!
KRAASH!
KA-BOOM!
TOY FACTORY

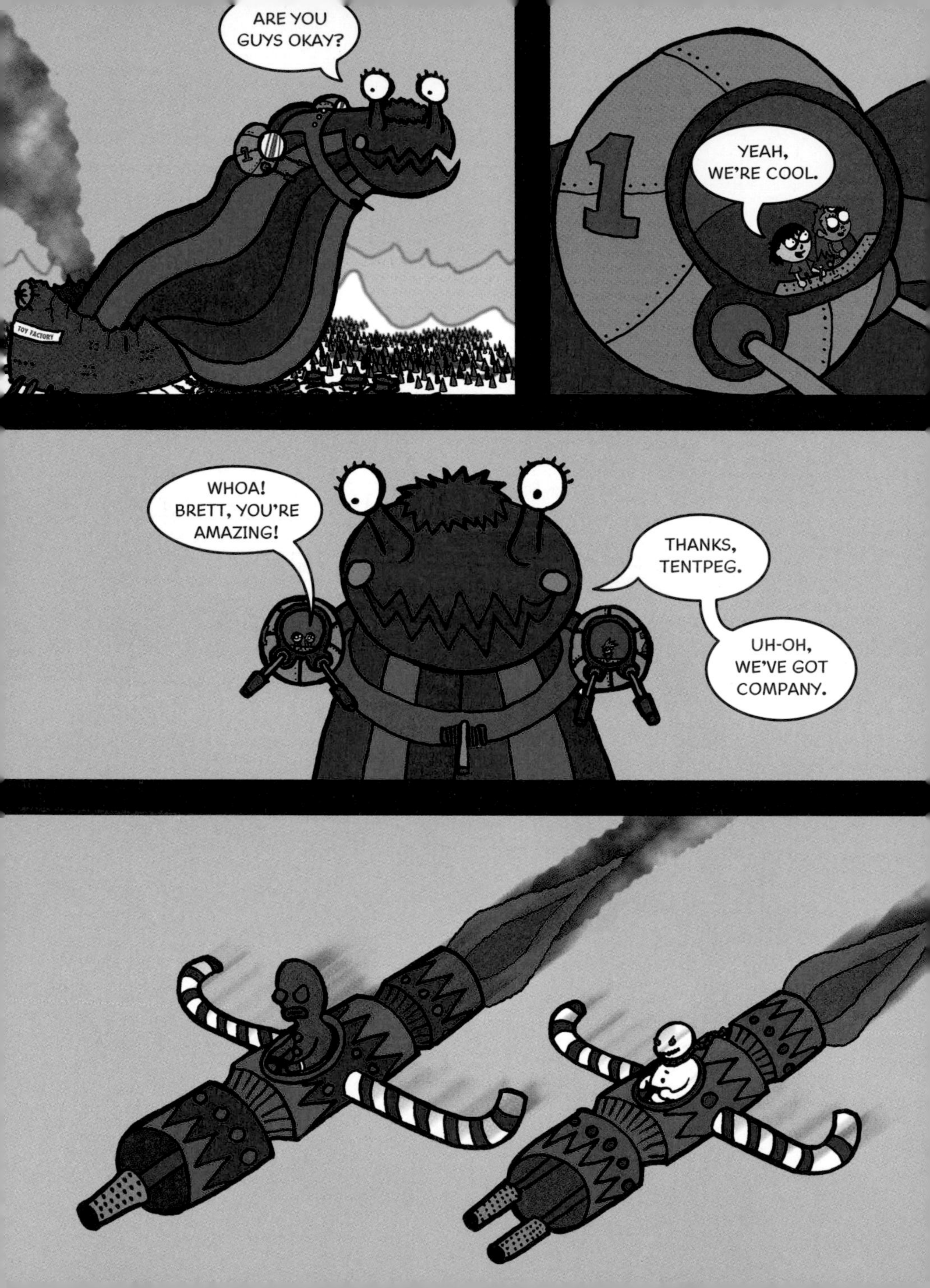
ARE YOU GUYS OKAY?
TOY FACTORY
YEAH, WE'RE COOL.
WHOA! BRETT, YOU'RE AMAZING!
THANKS, TENTPEG.
UH-OH, WE'VE GOT COMPANY.

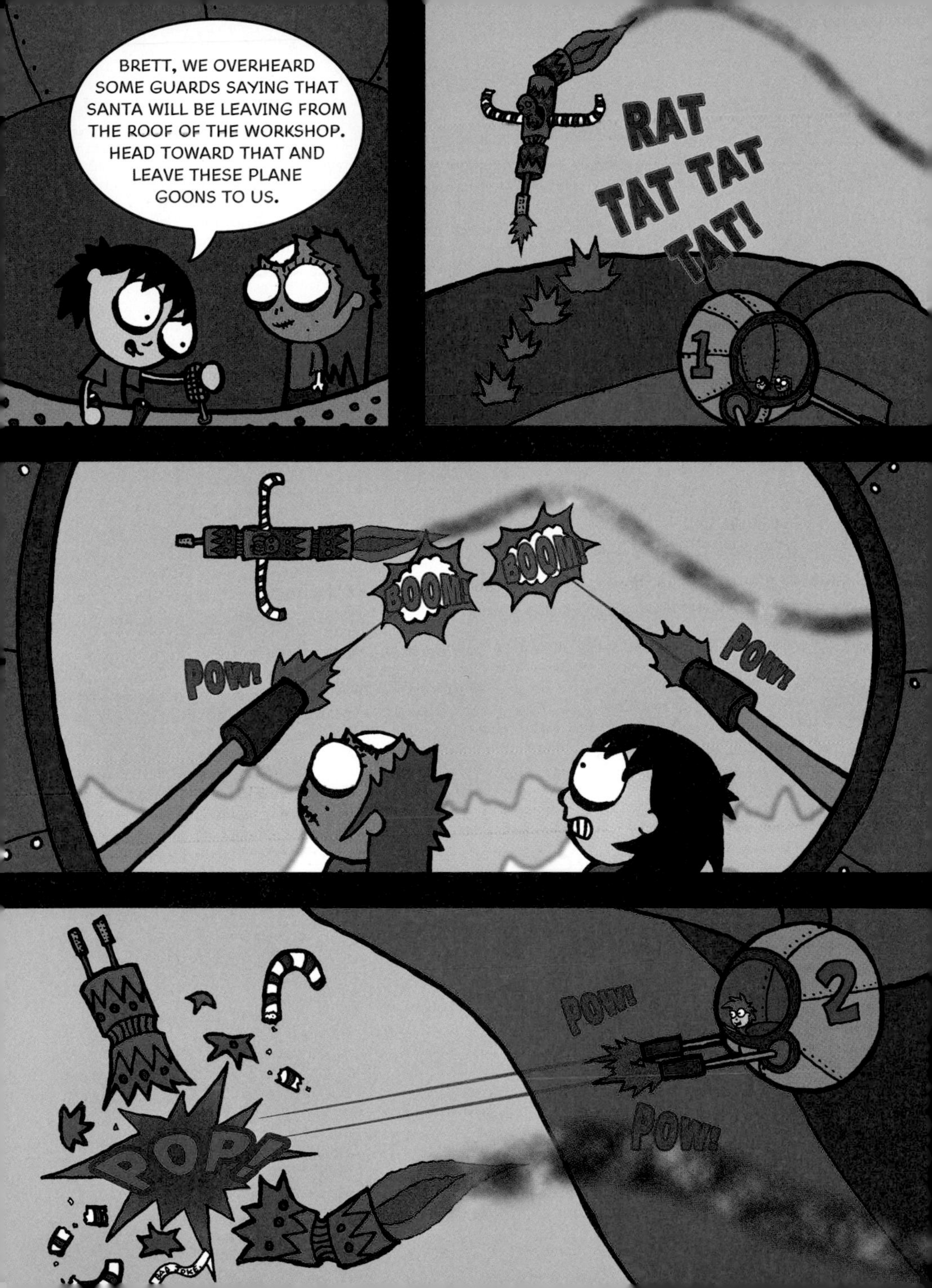
BRETT, WE OVERHEARD SOME GUARDS SAYING THAT SANTA WILL BE LEAVING FROM THE ROOF OF THE WORKSHOP. HEAD TOWARD THAT AND LEAVE THESE PLANE GOONS TO US.
RAT TAT TAT TAT!
1
BOOM!
BOOM!
POW!
POW!
POW!
POW!
2
POP!

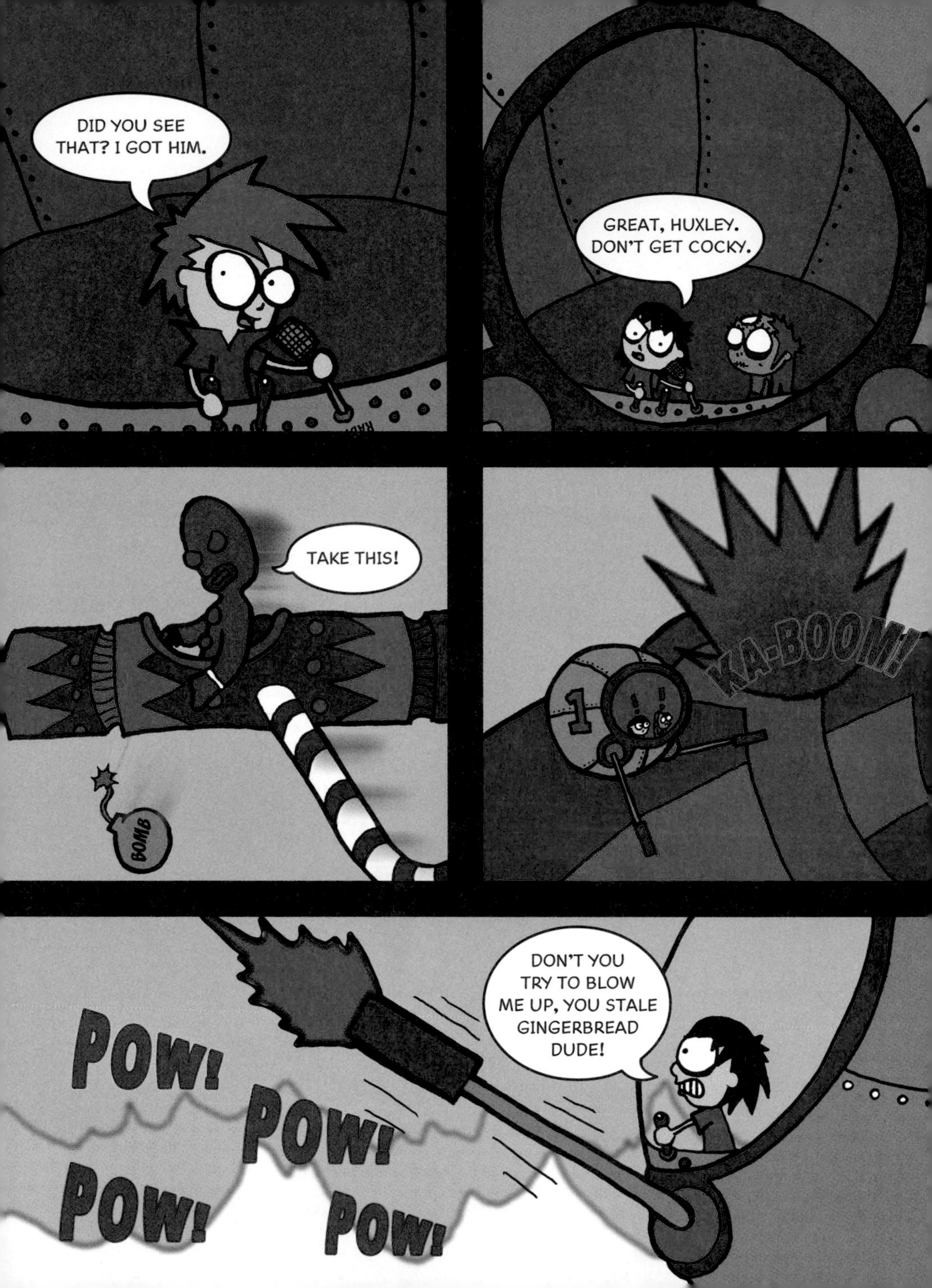
DID YOU SEE THAT? I GOT HIM.
GREAT, HUXLEY. DON'T GET COCKY.
TAKE THIS!
BOMB
1
KA-BOOM!
DON'T YOU TRY TO BLOW ME UP, YOU STALE GINGERBREAD DUDE!
POW!
POW!
POW!
POW!

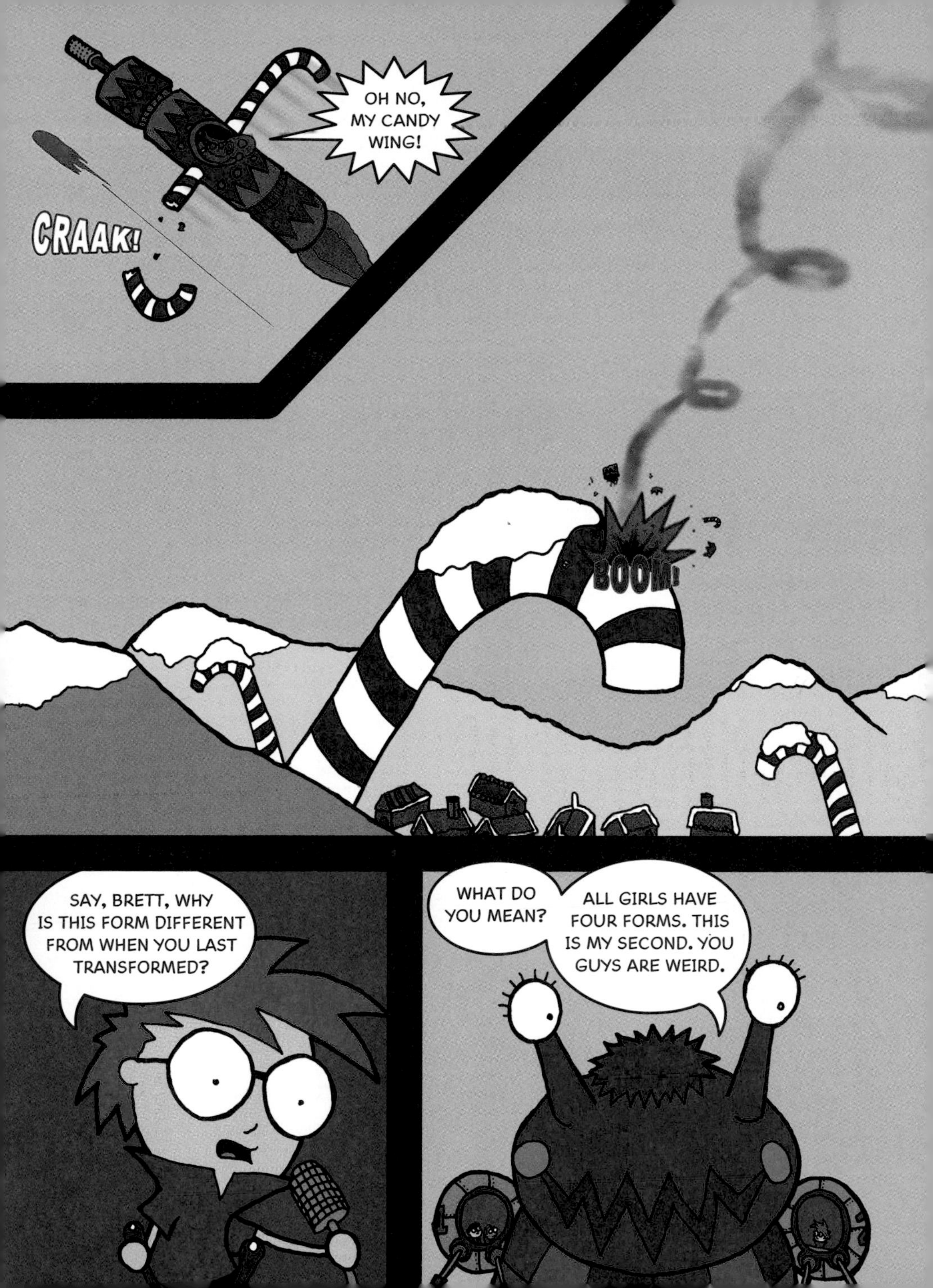
OH NO, MY CANDY WING!
CRAAK!
BOOM!
SAY, BRETT, WHY IS THIS FORM DIFFERENT FROM WHEN YOU LAST TRANSFORMED?
WHAT DO YOU MEAN?
ALL GIRLS HAVE FOUR FORMS. THIS IS MY SECOND. YOU GUYS ARE WEIRD.

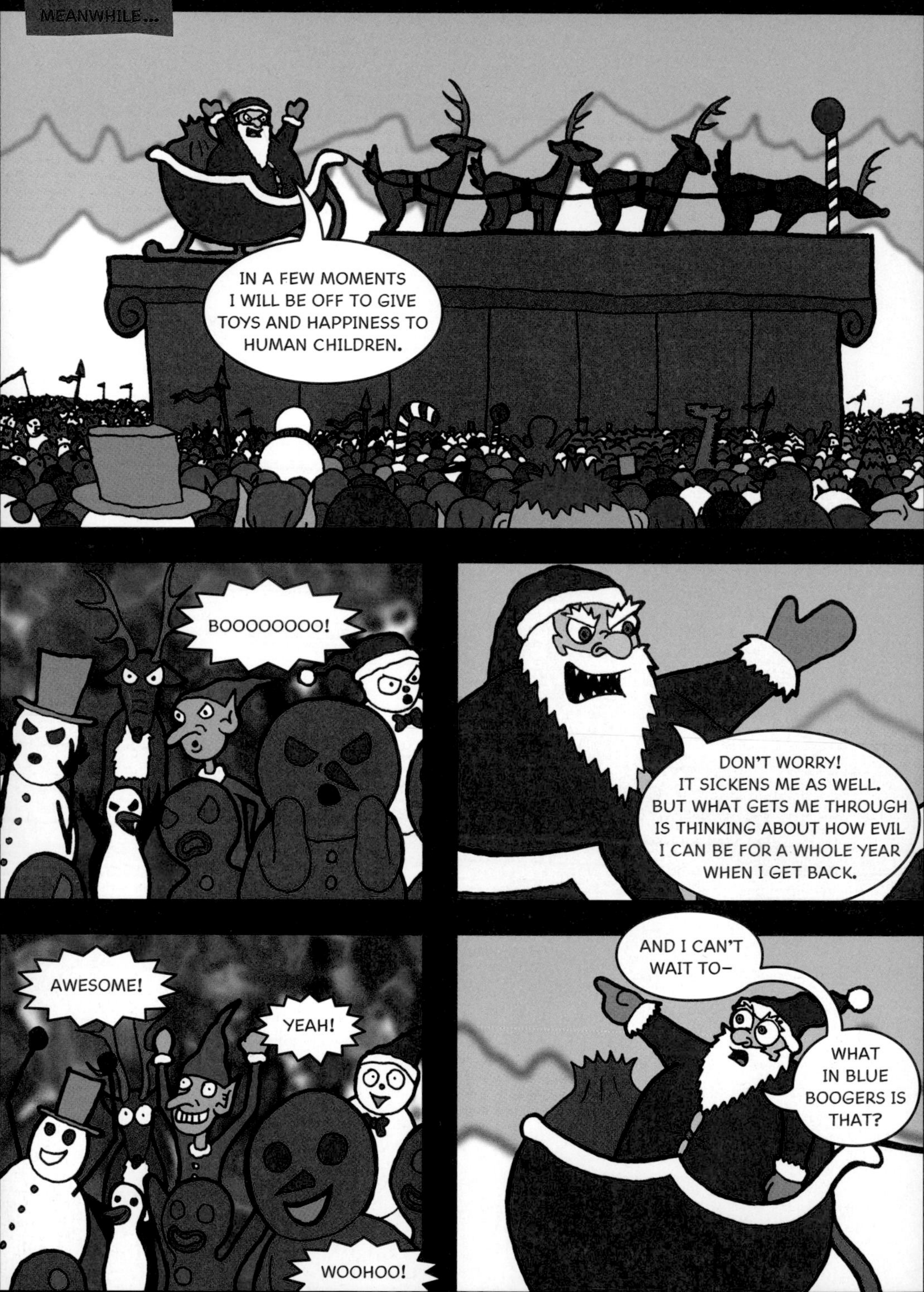
MEANWHILE...
IN A FEW MOMENTS I WILL BE OFF TO GIVE TOYS AND HAPPINESS TO HUMAN CHILDREN.
BOOOOOOOO!
DON'T WORRY! IT SICKENS ME AS WELL. BUT WHAT GETS ME THROUGH IS THINKING ABOUT HOW EVIL I CAN BE FOR A WHOLE YEAR WHEN I GET BACK.
AWESOME!
YEAH!
WOOHOO!
AND I CAN'T WAIT TO–
WHAT IN BLUE BOOGERS IS THAT?

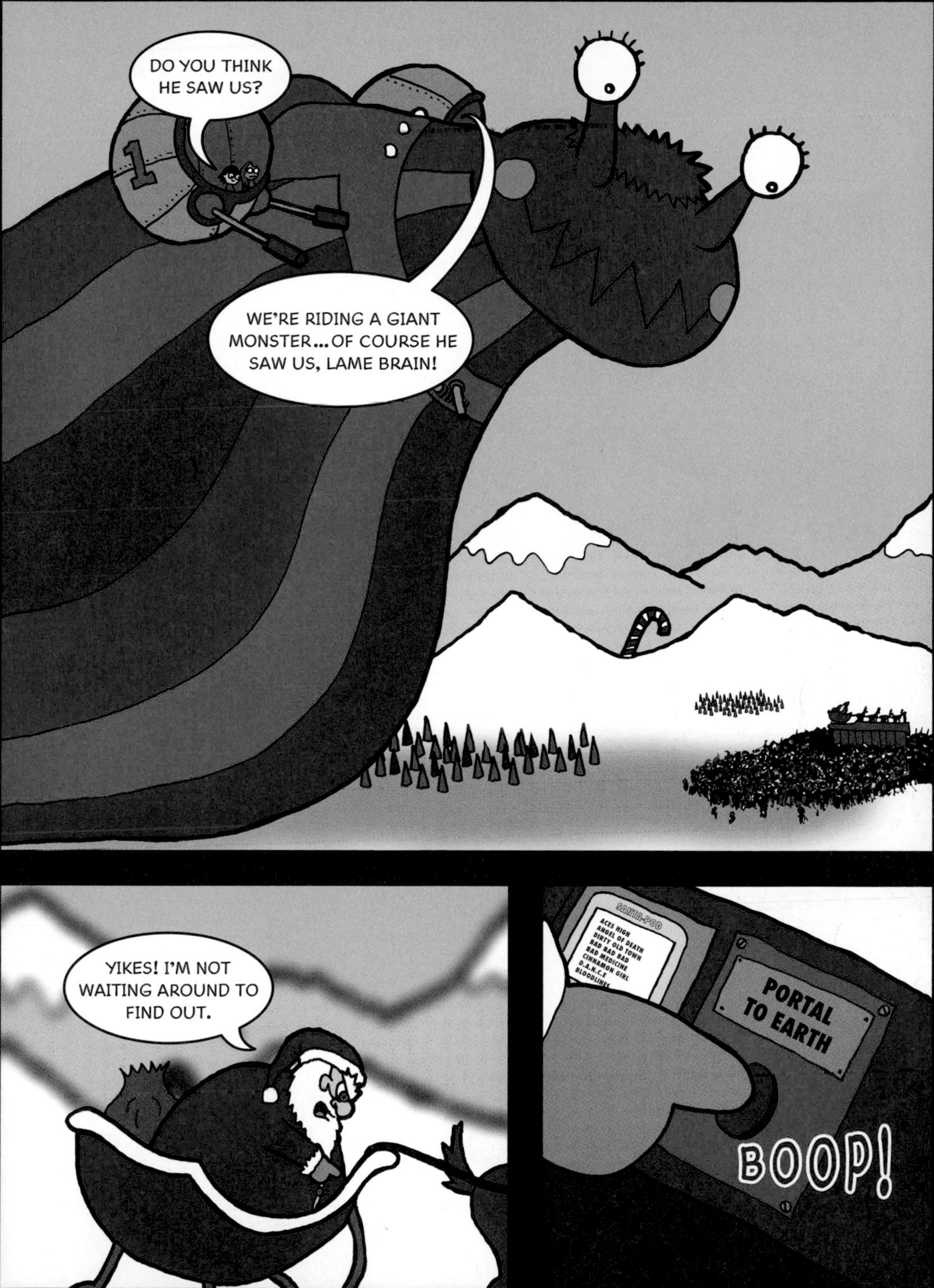
DO YOU THINK HE SAW US?
WE'RE RIDING A GIANT MONSTER...OF COURSE HE SAW US, LAME BRAIN!
YIKES! I'M NOT WAITING AROUND TO FIND OUT.
SANTA-POD
ACES HIGH
ANGEL OF DEATH
DIRTY OLD TOWN
BAD BAD BAD
BAD MEDICINE
CINNAMON GIRL
D.A.N.C.E
BLOODLINES
PORTAL TO EARTH
BOOP!

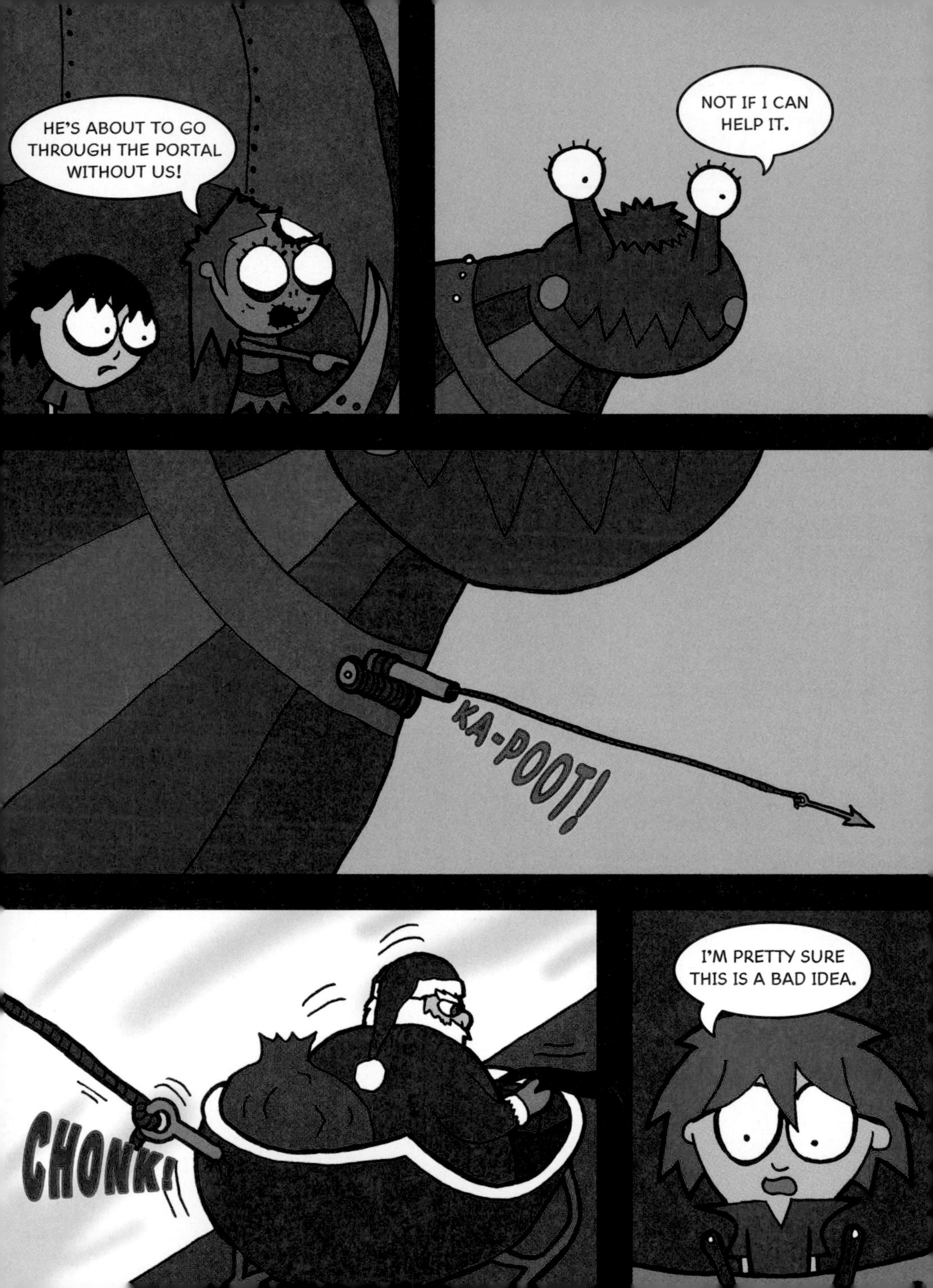
HE'S ABOUT TO GO THROUGH THE PORTAL WITHOUT US!
NOT IF I CAN HELP IT.
KA-POOT!
CHONK!
I'M PRETTY SURE THIS IS A BAD IDEA.

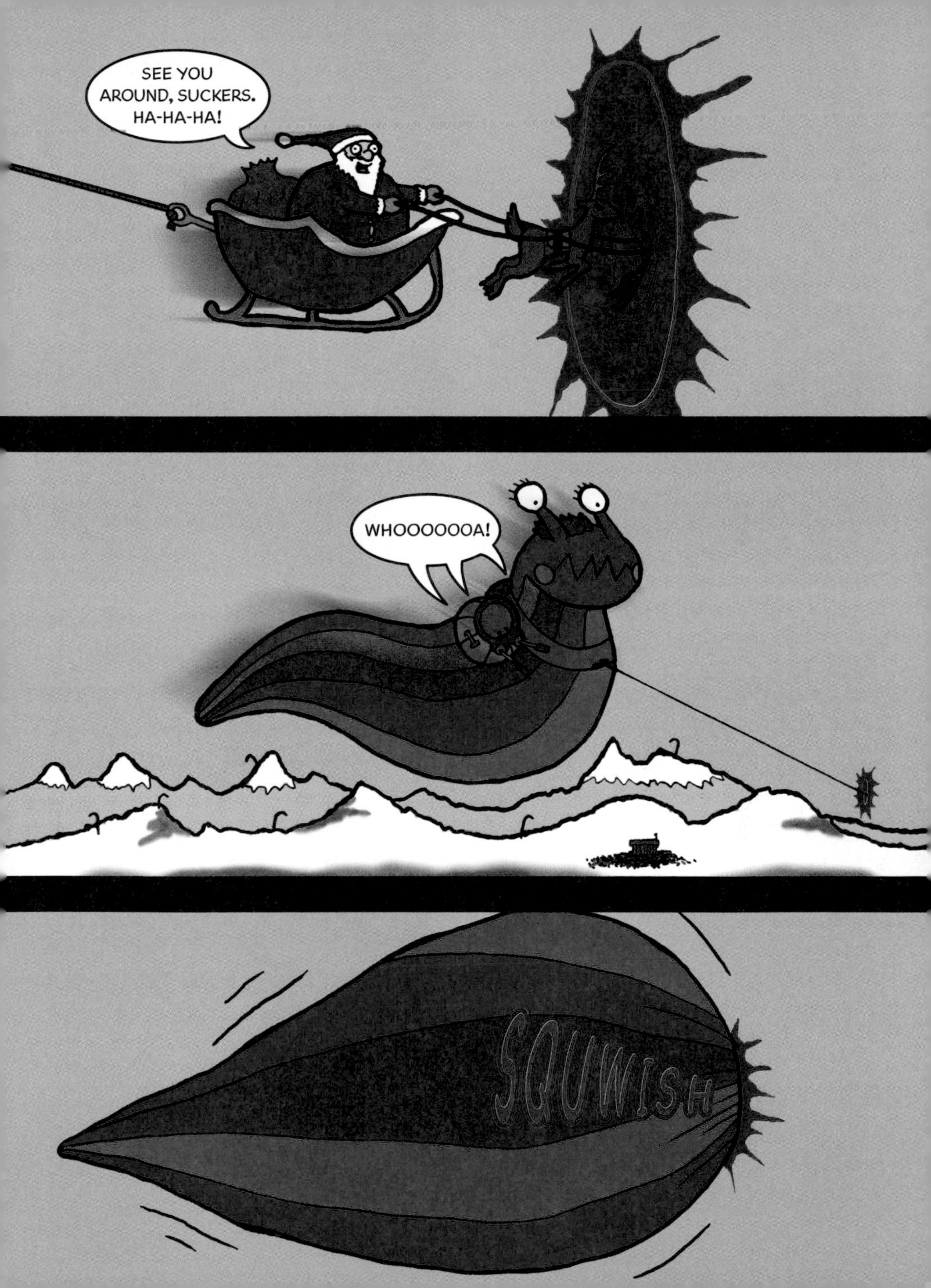
SEE YOU AROUND, SUCKERS. HA-HA-HA!
WHOOOOOOA!
SQUWISH

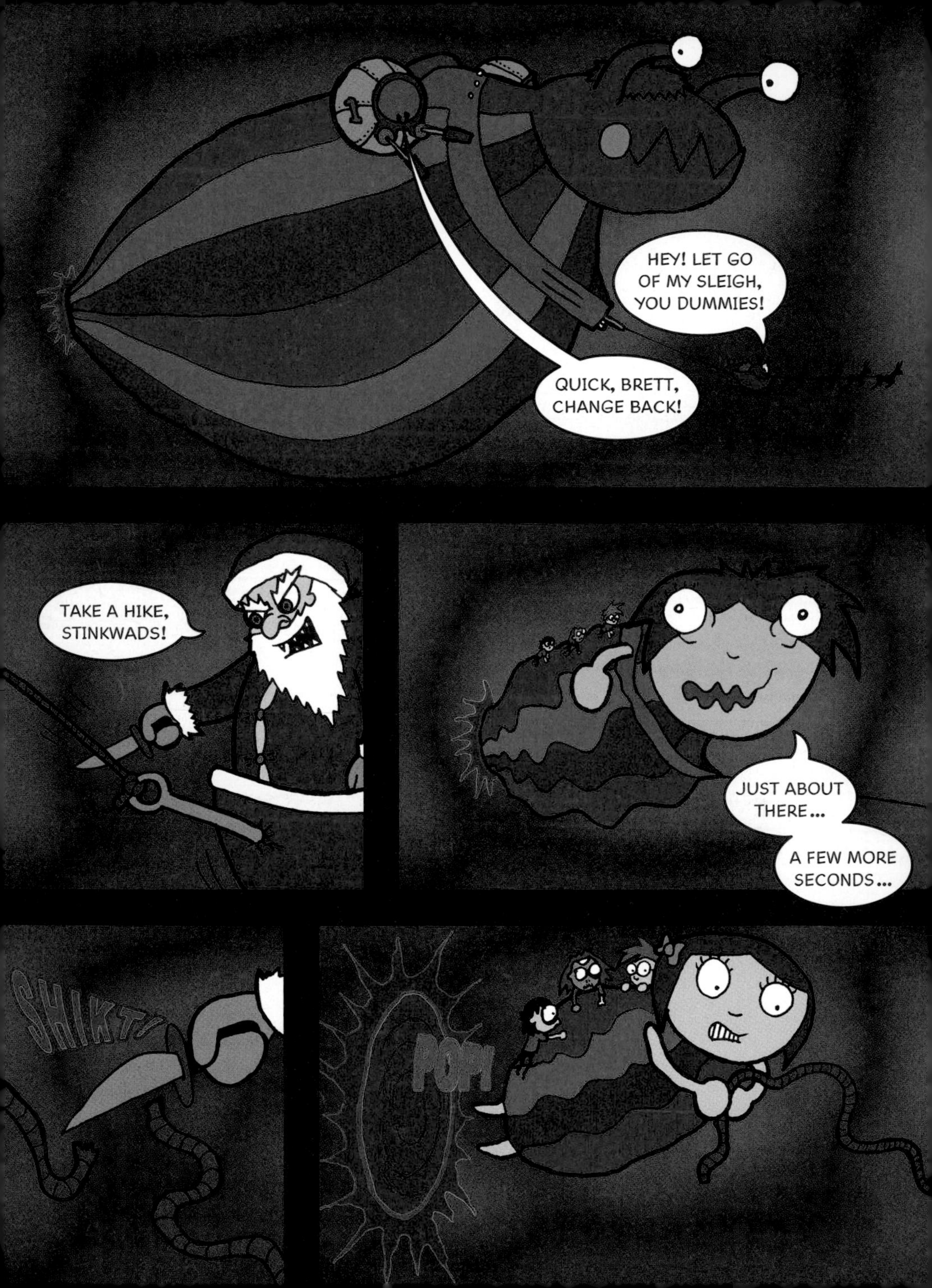
HEY! LET GO OF MY SLEIGH, YOU DUMMIES!
QUICK, BRETT, CHANGE BACK!
TAKE A HIKE, STINKWADS!
JUST ABOUT THERE...
A FEW MORE SECONDS...
SHIKT!
POP!

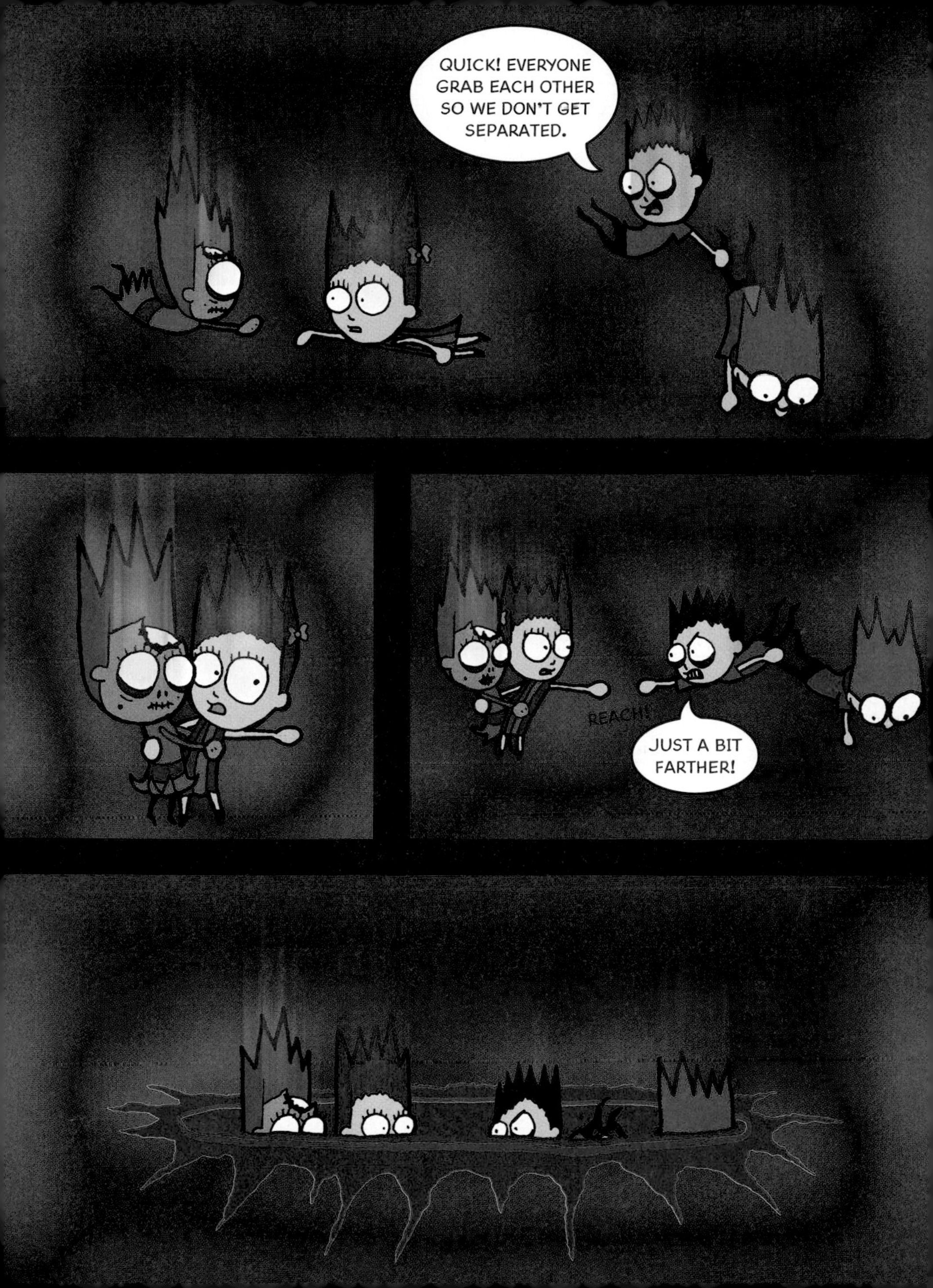
QUICK! EVERYONE GRAB EACH OTHER SO WE DON'T GET SEPARATED.
REACH!
JUST A BIT FARTHER!

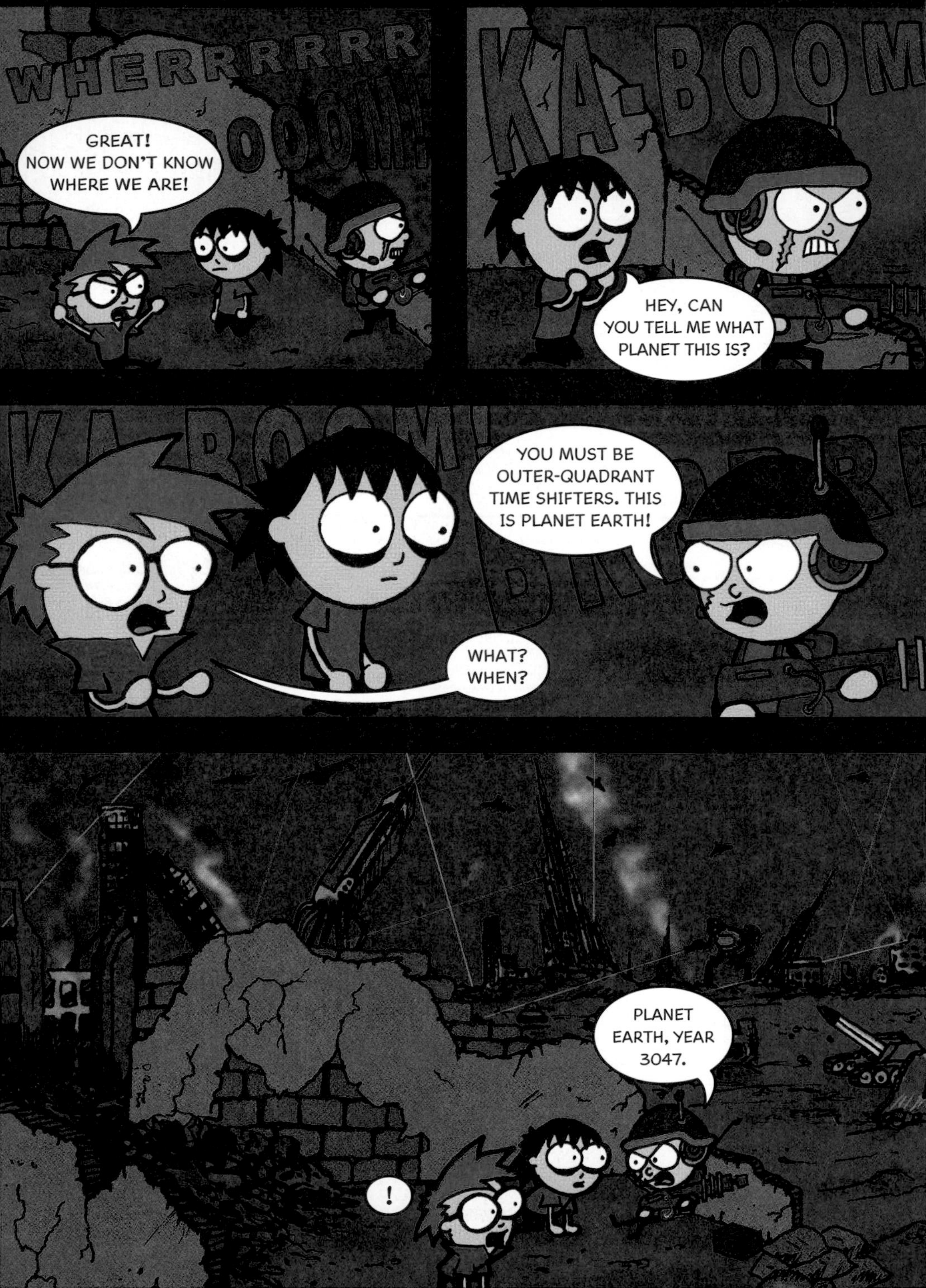
WHERRRRRR
GREAT! NOW WE DON'T KNOW WHERE WE ARE!
KA-BOOM
HEY, CAN YOU TELL ME WHAT PLANET THIS IS?
KA-BOOM!
YOU MUST BE OUTER-QUADRANT TIME SHIFTERS. THIS IS PLANET EARTH!
WHAT? WHEN?
PLANET EARTH, YEAR 3047.
!

AFTERWORD

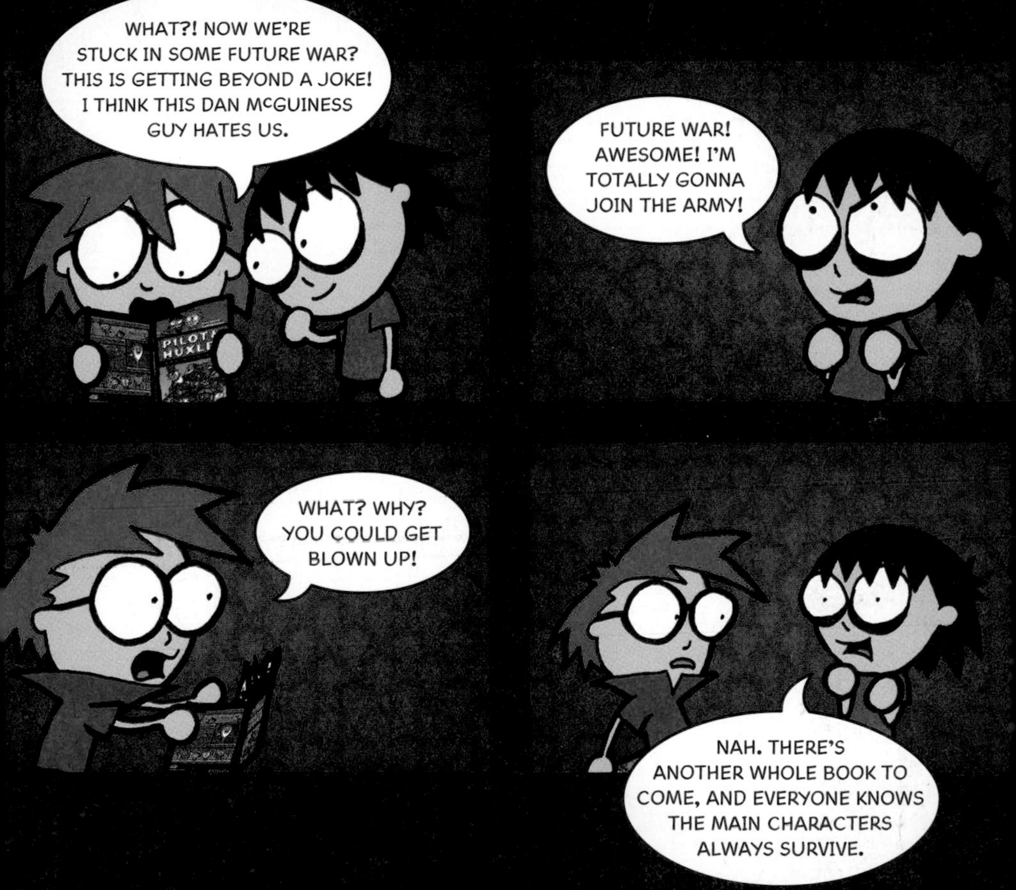
WHAT?! NOW WE'RE STUCK IN SOME FUTURE WAR? THIS IS GETTING BEYOND A JOKE! I THINK THIS DAN McGUINESS GUY HATES US.
PILOT & HUXLEY
FUTURE WAR! AWESOME! I'M TOTALLY GONNA JOIN THE ARMY!
WHAT? WHY? YOU COULD GET BLOWN UP!
NAH. THERE'S ANOTHER WHOLE BOOK TO COME, AND EVERYONE KNOWS THE MAIN CHARACTERS ALWAYS SURVIVE.

LOOK OUT FOR PILOT & HUXLEY IN THEIR NEXT ADVENTURE!

ABOUT THE AUTHOR

DAN GREW UP UNDER CLOSE SCRUTINY IN A
MILITARY FACILITY OF UNCERTAIN LOCATION.

THE MILITARY WAS TRYING TO HARNESS
HIS AMAZING POWERS OF RADNESS. THEN
ONE DAY AN EXPERIMENT WENT WRONG,
GIVING DAN THE ABILITY TO COMMUNICATE
TELEPATHICALLY WITH CATS.

UNBEKNOWNST TO HIS CAPTORS, DAN
FORMED A SECRET ARMY OF STRAY CATS.

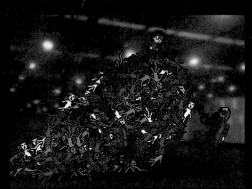

DAN USED THE CAT ARMY TO BREAK
OUT OF THE MILITARY FACILITY.

AFTER THEIR DRAMATIC ESCAPE, DAN AND
THE CATS WENT INTO BUSINESS WRITING
BOOKS. THE BOOK YOU'VE JUST READ
IS ONE OF THESE.